SPE[illegible]DERS

THE ULVERSCROFT FOUNDATION
(registered UK charity number 264873)
was established in 1972 to provide funds for research, diagnosis and treatment of eye diseases. Examples of major projects funded by the Ulverscroft Foundation are:-

- The Children's Eye Unit at Moorfields Eye Hospital, London
- The Ulverscroft Children's Eye Unit at Great Ormond Street Hospital for Sick Children
- Funding research into eye diseases and treatment at the Department of Ophthalmology, University of Leicester
- The Ulverscroft Vision Research Group, Institute of Child Health
- Twin operating theatres at the Western Ophthalmic Hospital, London
- The Chair of Ophthalmology at the Royal Australian College of Ophthalmologists

You can help further the work of the Foundation by making a donation or leaving a legacy. Every contribution is gratefully received. If you would like to help support the Foundation or require further information, please contact:

THE ULVERSCROFT FOUNDATION
The Green, Bradgate Road, Anstey
Leicester LE7 7FU, England
Tel: (0116) 236 4325

vebsite: www.foundation.ulverscroft.com

Mark Neilson is a former academic living in Perth, Scotland. He has written features and fiction for a variety of magazines over the last twenty years.

THE WIND FROM THE SEA

After the First World War, two final stragglers return to North East Scotland to pick up their old lives: Mary Cowie, once a 'gutter quine' or fish gutter, who served with the Elsie Inglis Scottish Women's Hospitals field units; and Neil Findlay, once the best fishing boat skipper in Buckie, now a shell-shocked wreck. They hope the old life will cure them, but find they have changed too much to settle down again. The shadow of the war refuses to go away for many of the other village locals as well. But with change comes opportunity, and Mary and Neil will soon find their tribal and personal loyalties tested to the full as Buckie struggles to move on.

Books by Mark Neilson
Published by Ulverscroft:

THE VALLEY OF THE VINES
A STRANGE INHERITANCE
ANOTHER CHANCE, ANOTHER LIFE

MARK NEILSON

THE WIND FROM THE SEA

Complete and Unabridged

ULVERSCROFT
Leicester

First published in Great Britain in 2017 by
Robert Hale
an imprint of The Crowood Press Ltd
Wiltshire

First Large Print Edition
published 2018
by arrangement with
The Crowood Press Ltd
Wiltshire

A catalogue record for this book is available from the British Library.

ISBN 978–1–4448–3589–2

To Pat

For all the hours you have spent alone while I was writing

1

Clouds pressed on the sea's horizon, turning it into a solid bar of black. Out on the pier head, the wind had an edge that cut through everything, and brought heavy seas thudding into the sheltering walls. It was May, almost summertime — but nobody had told the Buckie weather that.

Mary Cowie drew the old woollen jacket more firmly about her shoulders, and breathed deeply. She was back where she belonged. The wind from the sea biting deep into her lungs, driving away the smells of disinfectant and sickness, while the calls of the seabirds wheeling overhead drowned the memory of men crying out in fear and pain. She had come home, from the war. To start out in life again.

A gust of wind whipped dark hair around her face. Absentmindedly, she tried to tuck it beneath the jacket's hood — then gave up and threw her head back as the wind streamed round her. The thought of this moment had kept her going, been her talisman through five years in front line hospital units, then in the convalescent hospital back in England after the war had finished.

She leaned into the wind, like a carved figurehead on an old schooner, drinking in the keen fresh air. Then shuddered, wrapped the jacket around herself again, and began to retrace her steps to the inner harbour.

'That's never Mary Cowie?' A young fisherman paused in the act of mending his nets, looking up from the deck of his boat. Dark curls spilled over his weather-burned face and bright blue eyes.

Mary smiled. 'Trust you to be the first to see me, Andy. Yes, I'm back home, at last — the prodigal daughter returned.'

He grinned. 'Don't expect a fatted calf. The way the fishing's been, a couple of stale salt herrings are as much as we can run to. What's kept you so long?'

'I've been working down south. Nursing the boys who came back from the war on a hospital train.'

He pulled a face, and began to stitch the nets again.

Amazing how quickly people wanted to forget the war, she thought bleakly. Above all else, forget the casualties who now made them feel uncomfortable.

'Home for good? Or just visiting?' he called up.

'I've done my shift at nursing,' she said. 'So I am here to stay. Wild horses couldn't drag me away again.'

'That's fine. I've missed you. All the young lads have been missing you.'

'Away with your blethers!' she laughed. 'I'm old enough to be their mother.'

He tilted his head, smiling. 'You don't look it,' he judged. 'Not yet.'

She picked up a piece of dried seaweed from the quay, and threw it down at him. He ducked, laughing, as it drifted down into the harbour water between them.

'Where's your brother, Neil?' she asked.

Andy's face sobered. Closed up, almost. 'Like you, he's late back.'

'Working somewhere else?'

'No. In hospital.'

'Oh.' She waited, but nothing else was volunteered. 'In hospital' could mean anything — or nothing. Lots of lads had hung back, to keep their wounded mates company. Even to help hard-pressed staff, as porters. 'Good to see you anyway, Andy. Tell Neil I was asking for him, next time you write.'

The head dropped back down over his nets. 'I'm not one for writing.'

She nodded. Like most local men, Andy Findlay had left school at twelve with nothing in his head but a desire to get out on his father's fishing boat, following his brother Neil. Most fishing boats were family-run, sons taking over when the father retired as skipper. As Neil had done, then gone on to prove his worth — a new skipper, inheriting his father's instinct for fish, sensing their every twist and turn in the sea. Catches meant wages, and men queued to work for him.

Old faces: the town would be full of them. She must drop in and see Aggie, a visit that would be something of a two-edged sword. It would be wonderful to meet her one-time best friend again: but that friend was now a war widow, with a young son who had never seen his father. Like plenty of others, in a Britain woefully damaged by the war.

That sick old war had a lot to answer for, she thought grimly. A lot of local lads had volunteered for service in the Gordons, then marched raggedly off to the railway station and a Pals' Battalion. Only a few came back to tell the tale. The rest were still in Flanders and the other battlefields: pushing up daisies, as the wounded survivors jested with their gallows humour.

Mary stopped, her face troubled. It was the future she should be thinking about, not the past and its scars. Lest she find herself reliving the old nightmares again, of a young

VAD thrown into front line nursing. Learning fast as she had to cope with the ongoing flood of torn and broken men and diseased wounds.

It was this omnipresent corruption which had driven her to transfer into one of the Elsie Inglis Scottish Women's Hospital's front line units, with their firm belief that the sooner nursing and surgical help could be provided, the greater the number of casualties who would survive their wounds. Whereas the War Office practice of shipping the wounded back to distant military hospitals with only primitive dressings on their wounds had meant that the filth of the battlefield had poisoned the damaged tissue, and gangrene was often a bigger threat than the wound itself.

She had suffered her fill of shock and horror. Now she was turning back the clock to her girlhood and her years as a young fisherlass. At the grand old age of twenty-five, trying to rediscover the joy and hope which that girl had once taken as boring and normal.

Mary looked across the harbour, up into the new town, which ran parallel to the sea front. There were figures everywhere; men wheeling barrows at the fish merchants' sheds, men lounging in doorways at the chandlers' and the sail-makers', filling bags on the colliers' quay, walking along past the seafront shops. Men and women going about their normal business. Living life quietly. As it should be lived.

She was home. Ready to remake her life and become a 'gutter quine' again, a fisherlass following the local fleet from port to port once the herring season started in earnest, gutting and grading the fish which were brought to her table, her hands moving so fast the individual actions of cutting, gutting and grading were simply a twist of the fingers and her wrist.

And the place to make her start was the visit she feared the most.

Mary braced herself. She would go and visit her once-best friend, the war widow with a new bairn hanging onto her skirts. Because Aggie, like herself, had to find a way to live her life again. Perhaps they could discover it together.

* * *

Nobody could mistake him for anything other than a soldier. From the close-cropped hair, greying at the temples, down through the granite-set face, the broad shoulders swaying to the regular marching stride, everything about him shrieked military.

His dusty boots pounded out the miles along the road to the Banffshire coast, looking as if they could march forever. From the dust of travel on the man's clothes too, they might have done that already. The wind moaned, the sun scattered shadows, the pulses of rain slanted down. The steady stride never faltered: this soldier had marched through a whole lot worse than this.

He turned, almost marking time as the inside man on an invisible file of soldiers, where a narrow road branched off down the shallow hill and dropped to the dark blue steel of the sea. Grey houses sat in neat rows down below him: the harbour lay behind these, he knew. Just as he knew there would be faces in that harbour, and in the tiny fisher villages that made up the town, there would be eyes upon him that he would struggle to meet. Because of the men who had marched with him up this road in another lifetime, as a ragged, jesting volunteer corps. The least he could do was to march their shadows back down the road, in silent, soldierly style.

The sun blinked out from behind a cloud as he strode through the first scattered group of houses in the new town that a laird had once planned above the sea towns and the harbour. Down to the start of the town proper, the tall, grey houses and the scattered shops. In the distance, seagulls wheeled and called.

He marched on, oblivious to the curious stares from the women entering and leaving the shops. There was something about him which was familiar, but it edged away from their minds. Just another soldier laddie, dropping in for a mouthful of food and a drink if he'd enough money in his pocket. On his long way home. A journey which a lot of their own Buckie loons would never make.

At the crossroads, among the horses and carts, a charabanc backfired.

It happened so often these days that few people noticed. But the soldier, at the very instant of the noise, threw himself into a rolling dive that took him into the shelter of a shop doorway, scattering the women there. Just as quickly, he was on his hands and knees, peering out round the corner of the doorway.

Tense as a coiled spring for a few seconds. Then his head drooped.

The man sighed, and pushed himself back to his feet, dusting down the well-worn uniform. Only then, it seemed, did he become conscious of the women watching, one with a small child clutching at her skirts, grubby hands to his mouth.

He stood up awkwardly. Raised his own hand, in mute apology.

Then with an effort that was worth a medal in itself, he straightened his shoulders, set his head back in the same granite-hard angle it had held before, and began marching again, down to the harbour. With a driven intensity.

Behind him, two women watched. 'Have you ever seen the like . . . ' the older woman said breathlessly. 'What got into the lad?'

'He thought it was the guns,' the younger woman said, her arm already round the child, offering automatic security and comfort.

'From the war?'

'Where else?' The young woman gathered the boy in front of her. 'And do you know who he was?' she asked. 'That was Neil Findlay, Eric Findlay's son.'

The older woman shielded her eyes. 'I'd never have known him,' she said. 'He's changed so much.'

'Haven't they all?' the young woman said bitterly. 'The ones who came back are all different men. But better different, than dead.' She stared after the marching figure. 'That frightened laddie was once the best skipper sailing out of Buckie.'

'Maybe he was,' the older woman said. 'But he's a sick man now . . . '

* * *

'I thought you said that the bread was stale,' said Mary, nibbling a sandwich.

'Even the seagulls turned it down,' smiled Chrissie Buchan.

'Then they're better fed than they were before I left,' Mary replied.

Chrissie sighed. 'Old bread's cheaper than new. With no man in the house, every farthing has to do the work of two. The local boys are good. Fishermen look after their own — especially the ones who worked with Tom. They drop in to leave us some fish, or old clothes for the bairn. They don't insult us with money — although there's not much of that around.'

'Has the fishing been bad? Andy Findlay said as much.'

'There were barely a dozen boats working from the harbour in the war — and there's only half the usual fleet getting provisioned for the herring season.'

The one sure thing about fishing was that the good years were more than balanced by bad ones, Mary thought. The whole community enjoyed the first, and tightened its belt to survive the second. Not just the fisher folk. But all the trades which supplied them, from the sail-makers to the coal merchants.

'Sounds grim,' she said. She hesitated, then asked: 'How is Aggie taking Tom's death? It's two years now, isn't it?'

Chrissie grimaced. She feared, as well as felt, for her daughter. 'She's taking it sore. She's left with a child who has no father, and no money coming in. Is that why you're here? To take her back to work on the fish?'

The old woman's eyes were shrewd, compassionate. The young woman in front of her had deep lines round her mouth and eyes, where there had been laughter before. The war had left its mark on her. And if she was back to stay, then she was back to work. In a fisher town, there was no other option.

Mary nodded. 'The Lord helps them that help themselves,' she said. 'I've dropped in to see if Aggie will make up a gutting team for the season. And ask if she knows anybody who can work as our packer.'

It was the traditional way of working: two women gutting and grading the herring, while the third laid out the filleted carcases neatly in barrels, and scattered salt to preserve them. Back-breaking work for all three — especially the packer.

The outside door clicked open and a gust of Buckie wind surged in.

'That's her. Ask her now. Aggie! We've a visitor,' Chrissie called through.

The door opened slowly: almost defensively. The child was pushed through first, with the mother following. She peered through the gloom of the cottage, then her whole face lit up.

'Mary! Mary Cowie! You've come home at last.'

The two women embraced. Aggie finally pushed Mary out to arm's length.

'You look older, quine. Nearly as old as me.'

'Fresh air and good food will sort that out. For both of us.'

'We can manage the air,' Aggie said drily. 'What brings you here?'

'To see you. To try and say what I couldn't write, about Tom.'

Aggie turned away, walking over to the sideboard where a soldier's photograph stood in pride of place. She touched it gently. 'Don't,' she said. 'Don't even try. There's nothing will bring him back. He was such a quiet and gentle loon — the world's worst soldier. Such a waste of a decent man.'

Mary walked quietly over. Placed a silent hand on her friend's shoulder.

Aggie blinked, tears filling her eyes. She had flooded oceans with her tears, yet still they came. She reached back, to cover Mary's hand with her own.

* * *

Mary set out from Aggie's house, and found herself down into the harbour again, instinct guiding her feet. She realized with a start that she had walked round the far quay of the inner harbour, out to the tumble of old nets which rotted there.

She shook her head in annoyance, and turned back. Then saw the figure of a man, sitting hunched up, with his head resting on folded arms. The nets were gathered round him — as much for a screen, she sensed, as shelter from the wind.

The nurse in her reacted before she had time to think. She walked quickly over, kneeled down. Gently touched the bowed shoulder, which flinched.

'Are you all right?' she asked. 'Do you need any help?'

The face came up, the eyes glazed. He had bitten his lip, she saw: and chewed the knuckles of his right hand, until they bled. He stared blindly at her, and through her — a look she knew only too well from the convalescent hospital.

Mary's heart lurched. 'Is that you, Neil? Dear God, is that really you?'

He blinked. 'Couldn't do it,' he said thickly. 'Couldn't face them.'

'Do what? Face who?'

'Everybody. All the mothers and the fathers, the brothers and the friends of the boys I didn't bring back home . . . '

As he spoke, his voice wavered, and his whole body began to shake. She saw the big hands grip his knees until the knuckles showed white. Without effect.

'Sorry,' he mumbled. 'Can't stop it. Shell-shock.'

'I know,' she said. 'I have seen it often enough.'

She reached out and firmly prised the big hands free, holding them in her own two hands and waiting until the shaking eased. Giving him the human contact that meant so much to men, when they'd got lost like this inside their minds.

He glanced up from hunched shoulders. 'You were there. At the war.'

'I was. And many's the time I wished I'd never seen France or Belgium.'

The shaking stopped. Head still down, he released her hands. There were white marks where his fingers had gripped. 'Came out of nowhere, the shaking,' he mumbled. 'For years, I was fine. Scared, but coping. Like we all were. Then one morning, I couldn't give an order, or even lift my own rifle without dropping it.'

The grey eyes came up, defiant and with something ironic in them.

'I'm one of the lucky ones,' he said. 'The generals shot boys that were far worse than me.'

'I know,' she said. 'From what I saw, it was the generals they should have shot, and saved the men.'

He laughed. An unsteady bark.

'Funny,' he said. 'That's what we thought too.'

She studied him. His eyes were calm now, steady and direct. 'Have you been back home, Neil?'

He shook his head. 'I'm not ready to see my dad just yet. Or Andy.'

'Where are you going to sleep tonight?'

'The boat's back there. I'll use the crew's quarters.'

She looked doubtfully at the moored fishing boats in the harbour.

He read her mind. 'The key has been hanging in the same place on the galley wall, ever since my dad took over as skipper. This isn't London, with its light-fingered folk. This is Buckie. The local grocer uses that same key to drop in our provisions. Everybody knows where it's kept. In fact, the key is probably hung in the same place on every steam drifter round this harbour. I'll be fine.'

She rose slowly. 'I could come home with you. Make sure you got there.'

'Oh I remember the way home,' he said. 'That's not the problem. Not even the start of it . . . You're Mary Cowie, aren't you?'

She nodded.

'I knew your eyes,' he said. 'Straight off, I knew it was you.'

What a strange thing to say. She found herself blushing furiously.

'You were a bonny quine,' he murmured. As if a thought had found words and escaped him.

'Your brother seems to think that I still am.'

A nurse quickly learns that a fast tongue is the best way out of trouble.

It brought a real grin. 'Andy hasn't changed, then. Of course you are — but inside, you are as lost and empty as I am. Aren't you?'

Mary hesitated. Then nodded. 'How do you know?'

The slow smile started in his eyes, and spread to the pale face.

'Because I was there too,' he said. 'In hospital. Just like you.'

* * *

Jonathon Bradley threw his doctor's bag into the small black car. Diabetes: he had known it from the first whiff of the man's apple-sweet breath. But how could you persuade a wife who had looked after him for nearly fifty years to change the cooking habits of a lifetime? And where would fisherfolk who were too old for the sea get the money to buy the fresh vegetables and fruit he needed?

The worst thing about being a doctor was when you knew what was wrong, but couldn't cure it. Could only wait for the later symptoms to come marching in, as a life wound down. One day, maybe, chemists would find a pill or an injection which fought this killer of the old. By then, it would be too late for Donnie.

'Damn, damn, damn!' he mumbled, then glanced up.

His face brightened. 'Aggie!' he called over. 'What are you doing here?'

She turned slowly, the young child clutching her hand. He saw her frown disappear, and watched a smile break out over a face that had been locked into lines of worry. 'Jonathon!' she said. 'So who are you killing now?'

He laughed outright. Aggie could always lift him from his cares. They had been friends from school, two kids from the opposite ends of the town. In her ready wit he had found someone who compensated his more sombre moods. Friends, long after their paths diverged, when he went on to study medicine, and she went off with the rest of the itinerant young women to work as a gutter quine. Following the herring shoals, from May to December.

'Most folk here treat me with respect,' he protested.

'Aye. But I know you too well for that.'

She came over, her brown eyes dancing. 'That's a fair stomach you are putting on, Jonathon. Are you stealing food from the poor as well?'

He grimaced. 'Most of them don't have the money to pay for my calls. So they pay me in garden vegetables instead.'

'And you hand most of it back,' she said. 'I know. The whole town knows.'

'Well, there's a limit to the number of carrots a man can eat.'

They stood, silent for the moment, enjoying each other's presence.

'Want a lift back home?' he asked. It was a fair way back to Buckpool, down on the west of the town.

Before his mother could answer, the four-year-old was inside the car.

'The wee devil!' Aggie exclaimed. 'He's mad on cars and horses.'

'So was I, at his age.'

'Get away! They hadn't invented the wheel, when you were a loon. Let alone a car to run on them.'

'Remember, if I'm that old, I was in the same class at school as you,' he countered. 'Getting belted by the same teachers.'

'I never got belted,' she smiled.

'That's because I always took the blame, for you.'

'You never did!'

'I did so,' he lied shamelessly. 'And the memory of it should be keeping you sleepless at night.' He cursed himself, as the laughter died in her face.

'Sleepless? Aye, I get plenty of that,' she said quietly.

'Aggie. I'm so sorry.'

She waved a hand. 'I'm as well climbing in,' she said. 'The wee fella will bring the place down, if I drag him out of here.'

He went round and swung the starting handle, then came back to climb into the car. 'Why were you walking, so far from home?'

'Trying to solve a problem that has no solution.'

'Want to talk it over?' They had always shared their worries. Why change the habit of a lifetime? He eased out on the road and drove off, in no great hurry.

Aggie stayed silent, then puffed out her cheeks. 'I've been talking to Mary Cowie. She's back from working down south in an army hospital.'

'Is she? And?'

'She wants me to go back on the fish with her. Following the herring, like we did in the past. Like me, she needs the money. And the only way to get money in a fishing town, is to work on the fish, if you're a woman.'

'It's a hard life. Working out on the open quays. Staying in ramshackle huts.'

'It brings in money. There's no man to work for me now.'

Her voice was flat; all feeling ironed out of it.

'I heard,' he said evenly. 'And me saying 'sorry' isn't going to help. So are you going to go off with Mary and follow the herring?'

'Don't know. Because I'm a mother now. Gutter quines are all single lassies — you can't go away for weeks on end when you've a family to look after. If I head off to Orkney, who will mind the bairn?'

'Your mother?'

'A bairn who has no father should be able to look up and see me when he needs me there. Not his grannie instead.'

Jonathon understood her dilemma. Edging his dusty car round a narrow bend between the fishing cottages, he racked his brain for a solution that might help his old friend. But she was right: there was no work for a woman, other than acting as a housemaid or working on the fish. And nobody ran to housemaids in Buckie.

'Something will turn up, Aggie,' he encouraged.

'If it does, it's more likely to be a bill than a ten-shilling note.'

Her voice was angry, bitter. Not the Aggie he remembered.

He drew up outside Chrissie's cottage. 'I'll keep my ears open,' he promised, 'and if I hear about anybody looking for a decent woman to keep their house . . . '

She looked across at him. Sometimes, it seemed as if he came from a different world, where reality didn't matter. Maybe life was like that, when you had money. The need to earn cash was gnawing away at her, worse than any hunger. It was that, or swallow her pride and live in penury, on others' charity.

'Somebody looking for a housekeeper, here in Buckie?' she repeated with irony. 'If there ever was, there would be a queue along the coast, from here to Cullen.'

His face burned. 'Aggie, let me try to help.'

Impulsively she reached over, patting the hand that held the steering wheel.

'You already have, Jonnie,' she said. 'Thank you for your concern. Now, Thomas, if you're not out of this car when I count to three . . . One . . . two . . . '

Jonathon watched them heading towards the cottage. Aggie and himself came from different cultures, from lowly sea town and posh new town. But she was his oldest friend, and these differences didn't matter a jot.

He *must* find a way to help.

He put his car into gear, and drove off in a cloud of smoke. In his mirror, he glimpsed the child wave after him. Sticking his arm out of the window, he waved back. Watching the road ahead, he didn't see Aggie's hand flutter in return.

* * *

'Well, are you sure about this?' demanded Mary.

Aggie scrubbed her face with a restless hand. 'I'm anything but sure. Only, what other choice have I got?'

Mary squeezed her friend's arm. 'The Wee Man will be fine,' she said. 'If your mum could bring up a whole family on her own, she will manage Tommy.'

'I need the money. But I feel so bad, going away for weeks at a time.'

'If you don't work, it will be even worse for him.'

'I know,' Aggie said wretchedly. 'It's just . . . it's one thing leaving him with her for an hour, even an afternoon. But for a month, or six weeks at a time . . . '

'I need to know, for sure. Before we agree the contract.'

Aggie nodded irritably. 'I'm being stupid. I haven't slept for nights, but there's no other choice. Let's get it over with.'

Mary pushed open the door from the quayside into the fish merchant's shed, where the office was a cold partitioned space separated from an even colder storage area. Wooden fish boxes were stacked everywhere with *Walker Bros* stamped on them — although nobody had ever seen the brother. The local legend was that Gus Walker had bought them cheap, when another dealer went bankrupt down in Yarmouth. Why not? His name was on them. Well, sort of.

She knocked on the half-open office door. Gus glanced up; tiny metal-rimmed spectacles balanced on a nose as long and sharp as a ship's prow.

'Mary Cowie!' he exclaimed. 'And Aggie Buchan too. Like the old days.' He came over to shake their hands. 'Are you wanting your old jobs back? Or have you just dropped in to buy some fish for the pot tonight?'

Aggie wrinkled her nose. 'Not if they smell like this,' she said.

Gus grinned. 'That's the boxes you're smelling,' he said. 'But it's barrels we'll be needing, for Orkney and Shetland. I'm bribing skippers to carry up both them and my gutting quines. All payment cancelled, if they lose the barrels.'

The same old Gus, with a heart of gold behind an outrageous tongue. Mary smiled. 'Have you any work for a couple of experienced quines?'

Gus pursed his lips. 'More elderly than experienced,' he judged. 'If you were horses, I would be asking to see your teeth.'

'The last man that tried went home on a stretcher,' Aggie said darkly.

'And deserved to,' Gus laughed. 'You need to ask me about work, as if it was a favour? Two of my best quines ever?'

'We heard a rumour that times were bad. Poor catches,' Mary said.

'It's more than a rumour, it's the truth,' Gus sighed. 'Since the war, the Russians and the Germans have been catching their own herring. That's lost us our biggest market. Now the Stornoway boys are saying that the spring west-coast fishing is poor again, like last year. Sure, I'm using fewer teams — but a lot of the young lassies got a taste for the towns in the war, and never came back. I'm two teams short. Your jobs are there, if you want them. Have you a packer yet?'

'We've asked around. But everybody's fixed up with teams. We wondered if you knew somebody . . . '

'As a matter of fact, I do. A niece of mine, Elsie Farquhar. Just a slip of a girl, but a hard worker. I've been wanting to put her with a couple of experienced lassies like yourselves, to take her under their wing.'

'Does she have a long back?' Aggie asked.

Gus grinned. 'She can reach the bottom of a barrel,' he promised.

Mary glanced at Aggie, got a fractional nod.

'Then it's a deal,' she said. 'Usual rates?'

'Paid at the end of each fishing.' Gus held out his hand. 'I've known you and your families since you were school lassies,' he said. 'I'll look after you, like I did before. Make sure you have a decent bed, and food. Handle any problems.'

Mary shook his hand, then Aggie. The traditional unwritten contract, which neither party would ever dream of breaking. That handshake was the bond that tied the three of them until the season finished down in Yarmouth or Lowestoft in distant December, when the herrings would freeze to their fingers.

'Right,' Gus said briskly. 'The local boys are leaving for Orkney tomorrow morning. I want you packed and here, for quarter to five. They'll take you up to Papa Stronsay, where I was short a team. That gives me a couple of days to find some other quines.'

'The daft ones are all spoken for,' warned Aggie.

He laughed, escorting them out, and patting Aggie's shoulder. 'Just like old times,' he said again. 'There will be plenty local lads, to keep an eye on you.'

It was another north east tradition that fishing families asked local fishermen to 'keep an eye on their quines' when half the town was living in a foreign port. The Orkney Islands and Shetland in June and early July, then sliding down with the shoals to Peterhead and Aberdeen in July and August. Down through Eyemouth in the late autumn, and further down to canny Shields and Yarmouth for November and December. With only a few days' leave at home between the fishings.

Outside again, the wind from the sea gusted over the bare quayside. Aggie shivered. 'We'll soon be standing out in that,' she muttered. 'And neither of us are as hardy as we were.'

‘Come on,’ said Mary. ‘I’ve a few shillings left. Let me treat you to a cup of tea and a scone in the hotel.’ She grimaced. ‘After tomorrow, the way we’ll smell of herring, nobody will let us in.’

They entered the hotel, and asked for tea and cakes.

When the tea was poured, Mary held out her cup towards Aggie. The older woman hesitated, then raised her own cup too. They gently clinked the rims together. ‘Here’s to us,’ said Mary. ‘A new start, all round.’

Into her mind there flashed the image of a broken man hiding out on a pile of nets, because he was afraid to go home. A man jumping at shadows still. Another lost soul, come back to his roots to try and find himself again.

She fought down an urge to raise her cup to him, as well.

‘A new start to us all,’ echoed Aggie. ‘I’ll drink to that.’

* * *

The old fisherman leaned on the harbour rail, puffing on his pipe. The last steam drifter had gone, her black smoke snatched by the wind and shredded in front of her, as she rose to the swell beyond the harbour. He had watched the scatter of local ships heading out, striking north. Watched until they were hull-down, below the horizon, each and every one of them.

With all his heart, he wished he was aboard and working again.

He took the pipe from his mouth, and spat expertly into the harbour below.

'That's a disgusting habit, Eric Findlay.'

He turned slowly round and smiled at the woman, then winked at the boy who was holding her hand. 'The spitting, or the smoking, Chrissie?' he asked mildly.

'Both of them.'

'I was just getting rid of the taste in my mouth. The taste of growing old.'

'And a bitter taste it is,' she agreed. 'But you're as fit and healthy as most men half your age. You should still be skipper of the *Endeavour*. With your boys to do the heavy work for you, and pick your brains when they can't find fish.'

'I'm too slow now,' he sighed. 'I'd drive Andy mad. He's always at the gallop, with his new ideas.'

'He still hasn't come near your own or Neil's best catch of fish.'

The old man pulled a face. 'Less fish in the sea, these days.'

'And less men to fish for them.'

Eric Findlay nodded. 'Has your Aggie gone then? Leaving the Wee Man tied to your apron strings?'

'And wet with her tears.'

Eric slowly fished in his trouser pocket for a silver threepenny bit. He held it up, made it disappear between two thick fingers. Then leaned forward and plucked it out of the child's ear.

'My, my! See what I've found!' he exclaimed. 'I wonder how many more of these you've got hidden down there.'

Young fingers took the coin uncertainly. Felt it for solidity. It seemed fine, although it was clearly a magic coin. He itched to reach up and check his ear himself. But he hadn't a hand to spare and, anyway, his mam was newly gone.

Maybe she'd be back tomorrow. He sniffed.

Chrissie put a comforting arm around him. 'That war has a lot to answer for,' she said bitterly. 'Among the living as well as to the dead.'

Eric nodded. 'Aye. It's finished off more people than it killed.'

'Your Neil?' she asked shrewdly, when he paused.

Eric shrugged. In a fishertown, everybody's business belonged to everybody else: there were no garden fences between families. A dozen neighbours had come round to tell him that his boy was back, before Neil showed up himself.

He fought to keep his face expressionless. It wasn't easy. It was the half light of dawn before the loon turned up. Not once had he met his father's eye. Neil, his strong son, always the steady one. Now his shoulders slumped, his clothes were dusty — even dirty. A tramp in the making. He had ached to reach out and hug the lad, but couldn't bring himself to do it. So he'd spat into the fire instead, and said: 'You'll be wanting your job back on the boat?' Neil had stood silent, then answered: 'I'm finished, Da, the war has done for me.' And he had filled his pipe while he fought back tears, then said roughly: 'You'll be finished when I tell ye that you're finished. Until then, you'll be watching that boat for me, and keeping an eye on your harum-scarum brother.' And had seen his reward, when the broad shoulders straightened.

Nobody as good as his son had been could be totally destroyed.

Or could he?

A dusty black car drew up, with a squeal of brakes. It had barely stopped before the child squirmed inside. 'Come out, ye wee devil!' his grandmother exclaimed, embarrassed.

'Leave him be,' laughed Jonathon. 'It's a seat that he's made his own already.' He glanced up from the open window. 'Eric, I spoke to my doctor friend down in Edinburgh, like you wanted. Can I see you on your own for a few minutes, when you have the time?'

The old skipper knocked out the dottle from his pipe against his heel.

'About Neil?' he asked. 'Fire away. Chrissie is my cousin, and has been out and in our house from before the boy was born. We've no secrets from her.'

Jonathon hesitated. 'Your decision. My friend runs Craiglockhart — that's a convalescent hospital for officers. The condition is well known and documented. It's a mixture of what my friend called 'survivor's guilt'. That's when somebody survives, while everybody else dies. The survivor feels that he has no right to live — that he should have died as well. It escalates into guilt — even into believing that you were responsible for the others' deaths. It's utterly destructive of a man's self-confidence and mental well-being.'

He paused, as seagulls wheeled and called above them.

'Add to that, for some men,' he continued, 'it just seems that the brain is battered once too often, by explosions and the carnage.

Their mind simply freezes, locks up. We have called the condition shell-shock, for want of a better term. It turns some men into rigid living corpses, and sends others screaming and hiding beneath the bed at any sudden noise.'

'Or diving into doorways,' Chrissie said quietly. 'When a charabanc backfires.'

'Exactly.'

The seagull calls above Eric's head were like the cries from lost souls.

He shivered. One of these lost souls was his son.

'And the cure?' he asked steadily. Skippers don't ever give away that they're scared half out of their minds. Not with the crews' eyes always on them.

'It's a new condition. We don't understand it, so we don't know how to bring about the cure. We can only wait, and see. Have patience.'

Blindly, Eric groped for his pipe and tobacco tin. He eased out a flake of the dark tobacco, and slowly ground it into crumbs between the heels of both hands, conscious that the other two were watching him. Feeding the tobacco crumbs into his tar-darkened pipe, he searched methodically for his box of matches. Struck a match and cupped his hands to shield it as he puffed away.

The great thing about a pipe is that it buys you time to think.

Even if thinking brings nothing. Other than an ache deep in your chest.

'Aye,' he said finally. 'Well, I have all the time in the world to wait.'

'You'll need patience too,' said Chrissie.

Eric turned, and spat to the leeward — the habit of a lifetime.

'It's not me that will need patience. It's our Andy. But patience, and him, have been strangers all his life,' he commented.

* * *

The steam drifter rose high as the grey/green wave flowed beneath the slim bows, then slid sideways, shaking herself like a wet dog. From behind the shelter of the deckhouse, the horizon tilted from one impossible angle to another.

Aggie gripped the deckhouse handrail. 'I hate the sea,' she said.

Mary held on with hands that were blue and red from the damp and the cold. 'Rich people go to sea for cruises,' she offered.

'If I'm ever rich, I promise you that I will never go on any cruise,' groaned Aggie. 'Is there any land in sight yet?'

'Over to the west, I think. Behind that bank of cloud.'

Aggie fought the spasms starting to build in her stomach. 'My old dad used to tell me about a deepwater sailor who retired, and set off walking into the dry bush country of Australia, with an anchor over his shoulder. When people stopped asking him why he was carrying an anchor, and started asking him what was that funny metal thing he had, he finally threw the anchor away, and lived the rest of his days in that scruffy little town. This morning, I can really understand why he felt like that.'

The drifter plunged, burying its nose deep in green water. They heard the propeller rise into thin air and begin to scream. There was a thud as the living wall of water hit the deckhouse sheltering them; then it was surging past, drowning their feet and legs in icy water and white foam.

'Aaargh!' moaned Aggie. 'Now my feet are wet as well.'

'Maybe we should go below,' suggested Mary, clinging to the rail with one hand, and holding Aggie with the other.

A crewman swayed past, whistling. His feet gripping the foam-streaked deck planks as if attached to them by suckers. 'A nice, fresh day,' he said. 'But ye'd be safer below for when we hit the Pentland Firth.'

'Does he mean that this gets worse?' hissed Aggie. 'Look, if you want to go below, feel free. I'm staying up here until . . . '

'Until what?' asked Mary.

Aggie was wretchedly sick, over the shining deck and her wet skirts.

'Too late,' she said. She turned a woebegone face to Mary. 'I don't know where we are, I've no idea where Orkney lies, or if we will survive long enough to get there. All I know is . . . '

She turned away, and began to retch again.

Mary reached over. With a frozen hand, she held Aggie's head, and comforted her until the spasm had finished. 'Better now?' she asked.

'All I know,' Aggie continued doggedly, 'is that nothing is going to stop me from getting there, and earning money.' She braced herself, staring out across the heaving waves.

'I'm not going home empty-handed,' she said. 'Not if it kills me . . . '

2

In high summer, up this far north, it scarcely got darker than twilight in Papa Stronsay. That made sleeping difficult in their communal hut, but gave plenty daylight for their early start. The gutter quines bolted down breakfast, and were waiting on the quay long before 6 a.m. It was cold, but not as cold as it would be later in the herring season. They were on edge, wanting to get started on the new fishing, and lose themselves in its constant pressure.

Mary checked the strips of rag she had bound round her fingers. The girls called them 'clooties', or cloths. They had a double use. First they helped you grip the slippery herrings before you started the single deft knife-stroke which sliced the fish open from gills to tail. Second, they were there to stop you from cutting yourself to the bone, if the razor-sharp knife slipped. At fifty herrings a minute, for long, cold hours on end, the mind tended to wander and the slimy knife became dangerous.

'Think we still remember how to do it?' Aggie asked ironically.

'It's like riding a bike. You never forget.'

'Aye. But I've never had a bike. Neither have you.' Aggie flapped her arms, generating body heat. 'That's the sixth time you've retied that pinny, Elsie. You'll have the strings worn out, lassie, before we start.'

Elsie flushed. 'I'm scared I'll forget how to pack properly.'

'Do it like we showed you,' Mary reassured. 'Just don't use too much salt.'

Elsie nodded numbly. How much was too much salt? Trust her Uncle Gus to put her with two of the best gutters in the town. She would never keep up. Then she'd be so clumsy she'd have the cooper scolding her, when he came to fit the wooden top into the barrel, then stamp it with the Crown symbol — to show that the herrings had been caught, gutted and packed within twenty-four hours. No rotten fish in here.

Nervously, she glanced along the table — a huge, scarred surface with tubs and barrels set out round and behind each team. The gutters cleaned the fish and graded by size. Her job was to take the gutted fish and stack them tight into each barrel. She had never been more nervous in her life.

In the distance, a bell struck once, twice, three times. The auction of catches had begun. Elsie swallowed convulsively. Out of nowhere, she found herself engulfed in a wave of homesickness and blinked back tears.

The gutting quines waited silently. Normally, they made as much noise as a flock of starlings. Girls from Ireland, the west coast of Scotland, all down the east coast, as far as Lowestoft. Places she had only heard about, from the men in her own family talking fish.

These women were a hardy independent bunch, with more freedom than most women knew in 1920. They worked as a group, looked after each other as a group, sorted out their problems as a group. No need for any man to step in and help. These women stood on their own two feet, and were proud of it.

Headscarves covered their hair. Thick cardigans or jerseys to keep them warm in all weathers. Oilskin pinnies wound round them, to keep off the fish slime and scales. While their feet were encased in thick Wellington boots, with as many pairs of socks as they could wear, to keep warm on the stone quay.

Elsie fidgeted, torn between wanting to get started and being terrified she would make a mess of everything.

Aggie understood, and slid an arm round the younger woman's waist. 'I mind the first time I did packing,' she said. 'For the first ten minutes, I couldn't see the fish for greetin'. Then my hands started thinking for me, and all I had to do was bend.'

'We've all had first days, and lived to tell the tale,' Mary smiled.

Elsie tried to return the smile. Failed. Then came a rumble of metal wheels on cobbles. The first wave of fish was coming to the different tables.

'Just dinnae rush at it,' said Aggie. 'Get these first two or three layers neat, and the rest will follow.'

One of Gus's barrows spilled its silver load of fish across the table. Herrings slid everywhere, piling up against the fiddles that kept them on the table.

'Let's get started,' Mary said.

She reached forward. Got the grip she needed to hold the slippery brute firmly, while the knife and her fingers did the rest. The razor-sharp knife sliced into the herring's throat, and down. The fingers following, hooked out the intestines and dumped them. The gutted fish was flipped into the empty tub, and she was reaching already for the second, and the third . . .

Too slow. She had never been this slow before.

A herring spun out of Aggie's hands, and leapt across the table.

'Is that one a salmon?' an Irish quine quipped from her side.

'If it is, then it's come to the wrong table. We only get paid for herring here.' Aggie reached grimly for another herring, taking an instant more to make sure she had the beast in a proper grip. Firm, without damaging the flesh.

They were desperately slow, all three of them. Falling far behind the flying hands of the seasoned gutters and packers round them. Then, by about nine o'clock, they stopped falling behind. Gradually, as the unending flow of fresh herrings to the table stopped overwhelming them, they began not just to hold their own, but to catch up. By then, Elsie thought her young back would break in two. And had lost count of the barrels she had filled.

Gritting her teeth, she packed on. Pulling her weight for the team.

* * *

'We need to set things straight,' Andy said. 'We've got to know where we stand.'

He leaned against the steering wheel as the drifter buried her bows in a huge white-laced swell. Solid sheets of green water flew back across the deck and exploded against the windows of the deckhouse. The steam drifter staggered, then its big propeller bit again and thrust her forward.

Neil wedged himself in the corner of the deckhouse. Once, this had been his second home. His hands, not Andy's, gripping the wooden spokes of the wheel.

The drifter plunged again. Another boom as the water exploded against her port bow. Another wriggle as, dog-like, she shook herself free.

Andy glanced over. 'I didn't want you here. That was our da's decision, not mine as skipper. With the bank threatening to take over the boat, we can't afford to carry any passengers. Not even family ones . . . '

He turned the wheel to port, meeting the next big swell.

'You shouldn't be on board,' he ground out.

Odd how the flaring temper of his youth had gone, Neil thought, leaving him almost indifferent to his brother's open hostility.

'I've no intention of being a passenger,' he said mildly. 'I'll pull my weight.'

'What if you get the shakes, when we are shooting nets or, worse still, hauling them? Leaving us one man short on the ropes and struggling. Everybody at risk — and nobody with the time to drag you into someplace safe.'

'It might never happen. And if it does, then it's up to me to get out from under your feet.'

'And be swept off the deck?' Andy demanded.

'My choice. My risk.'

'And my job to tell our da that I have lost you.'

The drifter lunged sideways, then soared up again. So normal, in these wild northern waters, that neither man noticed.

'You've got a full crew of deckies,' Neil said. 'Plenty hands on the ropes. The only job you hadn't covered was the cook. That's what I'm here to do.'

'The cook's job is always for a schoolboy,' Andy spat out.

Fuelling his anger was outrage that his ex-skipper brother was taking on the most menial job on the ship — and it didn't seem to bother him. It was Andy who felt the shame. It was the first job any lad was given, when he went to sea. The thankless task of making the galley fire and cooking basic meals, while the crew worked out on deck. Serving them, then washing up in a bucket of water drawn from the engine's condensed steam. But also to be on hand as the ship's dogsbody, throwing his weight onto the end of ropes when they were hauling nets, helping the engineer to shovel coal for the boiler.

First up, and last to bed. The harsh training given to any lad, and that harshness needed — because the sea was a far more savage taskmaster than any skipper and his crew.

Andy checked their course, and altered the ship's head a fraction into the waves. Light was going fast. 'It's going to be a right old job to shoot and haul the nets tonight,' he grumbled. His mind had already moved onto other things, because it's the skipper's job to think ahead. To guess where the shoals of herring would surface in the darkness. To guess what depth they would be swimming at and all of this on a dirty night, when there were no signs — like the phosphorescence shoals gave to the night sea — which would guide his choice. He was conscious that his record didn't match up to his dad's, or even Neil's.

That knowledge ate into him, like acid.

'Are we heading round behind the island?' Neil asked, as much a gentle prompt to his preoccupied brother as a question.

'Dunno. I'll see how I feel when we get there.'

The two brothers stared out at the rolling sea, and the low, grey clouds that whipped across it almost at mast height. Once the skipper had chosen the spot, it would take them a couple of hours to shoot their nets steaming quietly ahead and letting the sea pull the net overboard. Then they would drift silently for maybe four, or even six hours, before they began the back-breaking work of hauling in over a mile of nets. Shooting them again, if they were empty.

'I'd better be going,' said Neil. 'Make some grub for the men, before they start.' He waited until a wave surged past, then opened the deckhouse door.

Andy peered forward through streaming windows. 'Don't expect gentle treatment,' he warned. 'I'm treating you like the rest of the crew. Worse. So that nobody can ever say that I'm going easy on my brother.'

'I wouldn't want it any other way,' Neil replied evenly. Then closed the door, and stepped over the streaming decks, towards the galley.

* * *

'My nose is itchy,' Aggie complained.

'Want me to scratch it?' Mary held up hands that were dripping with fish slime and scales.

'How about these ones?' Elsie asked.

Mary saw that the young girl's hands were raw and red, from handling wet fish and salt. She felt pity, but there was nothing she could do to help. The damaged skin would toughen up — but never enough to cope with the agonizing hacks that all gutters and packers suffered, in the cold of the late season.

This was their second day of work, easier from the start. But the clouds were low and rain was driven across the tables by the westerly wind.

Aggie reached for another herring. With little more than a roll of both wrists, she had it gutted and dropped into a tub.

'Less fish been landed today,' she judged. 'The boats should get a better price for their night's work. The ones that found herring, anyway.'

Nobody mocked a boat returning empty-handed. It could happen to any of them. There was luck as well as skipper's skill in finding the shoals. But, since a share of what they caught made up a fisherman's wages, nobody sailed with an unlucky skipper for long. The crews, like the sea, were hard taskmasters.

Once the table was emptied, the women wiped their hands, and went over to sit on old boxes or barrels. Glad to take the weight off their feet, until the next batch of fish arrived. A few of them brought out their lunchtime 'piece', and started eating.

'There's Mary Cowie! Sitting like a queen.'

She looked up to see Andy Findlay grinning.

'So you managed to find your way back to the harbour?' she asked sweetly.

'Full of herrings,' he boasted. 'These fish scales on your nose suit you.'

Mary made no attempt to remove them. Fish mess was a way of living, when you were a gutter quine. She glanced beyond Andy, to see his brother standing quietly there. His eyes crinkled, and she smiled back at him. Glad that Neil had found his way back into the family boat and up to Orkney. In that tumble of wind and water lay his best chance of finding himself again.

The two fishermen headed into the village, for provisions. Most of the crews were catching up on sleep in the moored boats. They would be putting to sea again by late afternoon, ready for the night's fishing.

'I think that Andy fancies you,' Aggie commented.

'Andy fancies anything in skirts.'

'He's very good-looking,' Elsie said.

'There's more to a man than a head of curly hair,' Aggie replied.

She turned away. It came as it always did, a wave of misery that surged to overwhelm her. Two waves. First, for the loss of her man. Then second, her worry about what was happening to her bairn, back home. Was he missing her? Was he crying himself to sleep at nights, like she was doing? Or was he just too busy being a bairn, chasing other children, finding crabs in a pool. Climbing into doctor's cars . . .

Her lips twitched. He lived on impulse, that child of hers.

She looked out, over the roof of the auction shed. Jonathon. The friend from her childhood, who lived in a different world. Not that this mattered to them. They liked each other, and that was that.

She rose. 'When's dinner time?' she demanded.

'Here's Gus,' said Mary. 'Coming to check on his troops.'

The fish merchant strode up. 'What's this?' he complained with mock severity. 'My cooper's sitting against a wall, smoking his pipe and falling asleep. I'm not paying the man to sleep. I want him working. And that goes for you lot too. Get up, and fill more barrels.'

'Then send us some fish,' said Aggie.

'How's Elsie doing?' he asked, grinning.

'She's fine,' said Mary. 'Working harder than her uncle anyway.'

'That wouldn't be difficult,' said Aggie.

Gus shook his fist at them. 'I should never have hired the two of you,' he declared. 'My sense of judgement deserted me. You're taking advantage of my good nature. Setting a bad example to my niece. How are they treating you, quine?' he asked Elsie.

She blushed, to be the centre of attention. 'Fine,' she said.

Gus patted her arm. 'Aye,' he said. 'You could do worse than having these two for teachers.' As he turned to go back down to the auction shed, he added over his shoulder, 'But not much worse . . .'

'The cheeky devil!' laughed Aggie. 'Right. I'm starving. Let's have our piece, while we're waiting.'

'Is it not too early?' protested Mary.

'It's eat now, or forever hold your piece,' declared Aggie.

Elsie giggled.

'Don't encourage her,' Mary scolded. 'She got that joke from an Irishwoman, ten years ago . . . '

'The old ones are the best,' said Aggie, sinking her teeth into her sandwich.

* * *

The engineer paused from shovelling fresh coal into his bunker, wiping: a black face with an even blacker hand. 'Are ye better now, my man?' he asked.

Neil was every bit as filthy. His shovel lay discarded, as he huddled against the wall of the engine room. Shaking until his teeth chattered. It had come again, out of nowhere. Without warning. Mercifully, when he was down in the bowels of the drifter, away from the crew's eyes. More important still, out of Andy's sight.

He gripped his knees, until the shaking eased.

Then forced himself back onto his feet, picking up the filthy shovel. 'Don't tell Andy,' he mumbled. 'I'm depending on you, Padraig.'

'Why should I? Your food's on time. It's better cooked than usual. You're the first clean cook I've ever known. And you do your shift down here, on the coal, without a word of blasphemy. Why should I complain?'

They worked together, moving the fresh coal into the forward bunker, where it was easily shovelled into the furnace when at sea. 'I was at the Somme,' the engineer said suddenly. 'Got invalided out with shrapnel.'

Neil nodded. With shrapnel flying, most men picked up a wound from that instead of spent bullets falling. Unless you were running into crossfire from German machine guns. 'The Somme was bad,' he murmured.

'Had a mate who was buried alive,' Padraig

said. 'Shell landed, behind our trench. Blew the back wall in. He was screaming mad, by the time we dug his face clear. Finished up like you. We covered up for him, or he'd have been shot.'

He paused again, wiping a shiny black face with its white rivulets of sweat.

'You were a sergeant, weren't you, Neil?'

'I was.'

'You looked after your men?'

'I tried to.'

'Were any of them ever buried alive on you?'

'Aye. We dug for them, against the clock, with our bare hands.' Neil stopped shovelling, his eyes fixed on the glinting coal. 'We got them out,' he said, ever so quietly. 'We never stopped, until we did. But not all of them were alive. Some of them were left in bits, and we saved as much as we could . . . '

The big Irishman clapped him roughly on the shoulder. 'That's why your shakes don't bother me. And, for the record, I never saw them.'

* * *

Eric Findlay stooped, knocking out the embers from his pipe against the heel of his boot. Raising the iron knocker of the cottage door, he dropped it gently. The noise echoed inside the tiny hall.

He heard Chrissie's footsteps approaching from the other side. The door opened — nobody used locks in Buckie.

'Eric! Trust a man to know when the kettle's on. What brings you here?'

Hauling off his cap, he ran fingers through wiry grey hair.

'Got a letter from Neil. He saw the quines, the other day. They're fine and comfortable. But the fishing's up and down.' Eric shook his head. 'There's a lot of boats whose owners are depending on the next two months. We need steady catches at a decent price . . . Wish I was up there, to help the loons.'

Although retired, his old boat was a constant worry. Fishing boats were owned by shareholders; a mixture of family, outside businessmen, and banks. Cash earned from a year's fishing was used to pay the costs: then, from what was left, each shareholder drew his share. In good years, fishing was a sound investment. In a bad year, you fought to cover your costs. Over a series of bad years, outside investors didn't just tighten their belts. They complained: quietly at first, then louder.

'Did Neil speak to Aggie?' Chrissie broke into his thoughts. 'How's she coping with . . . you know . . . ' She nodded silently down towards the child at her side.

Eric felt in his pocket, and hid another silver three-penny bit between his fingers. Silently, he showed the empty hand to Tommy. Then reached forward and plucked the small silver coin from the boy's ear.

'You want to watch that granny of yours,' he said. 'That's another thrupp'ny bit I saw glinting in your ear. She should wash them cleaner . . . '

As the child turned over the small coin, Eric glanced at Chrissie. 'When Neil saw Aggie, she was eating a sandwich at barely nine o'clock in the morning. He says she was giving as good as she got from Gus.'

'He's got a heart of gold, that man,' smiled Chrissie.

'And a tongue like a rasp.'

'But did he get a chance to speak to her? Ask about the Wee Man?'

Eric shook his head. 'He didn't say. Neil's not one for talking much — it's Andy who would blether away to anybody.'

Chrissie smoothed the boy's hair. 'She must be hurting,' she said.

Eric shuffled uneasily. Talking about emotions made him uncomfortable. 'About wee Tommy,' he said. 'There's a girr and cleek — you know, an iron hoop — somewhere up in the loft back home. Both the boys used it.

They ran for miles behind it. I wondered if he's old enough for that . . . '

Chrissie looked down. 'He's only four. Maybe it's too soon.'

Eric nodded. 'That's what I thought. Decided I had better ask, before I got myself stuck in the trap door to the loft.' He grinned. 'I'm neither as thin or as supple as I was when I stacked their toys away.'

'Waiting for the grandchildren?'

'More like to tidy up the house,' he said, embarrassed.

'It will happen. One of these days, young Andy will decide to settle down. Or Neil will find a quine whose quietness matches his. And before you know it, your cottage will be full of bairns running around again.'

Eric winced. 'A couple would do,' he hedged.

'Get away with you! I never saw a more natural grandfather . . . '

'Me? No. I'm ower young and irresponsible to be a granddad. I wouldn't know where to start.'

'You manage fine, with Tommy.'

'That's different.' He turned away. 'I'm off to the harbour for a smoke.'

'The kettle's boiling, through at the fire.'

'Another time,' said Eric. His body was itching for a smoke. Strange, he had never thought about the day when his loons would settle down. Another generation for him to teach how to fish.

He sniffed the wind. Cocked his head and studied the clouds. The wind would veer west, he judged. Just enough to rough up the sea, and stop it from being a window, letting the fishes see the boats that hunted them. If he was on that old boat, he knew exactly where he would go tonight. Fill his holds. Get some money in, to keep the bank quiet. He felt old, and useless. Groping in his pocket for the empty pipe, he rammed it into his mouth. Started searching for his tobacco tin.

He wondered how Neil was getting on. Always a tower of strength, out at sea, and then the war. Not any more. Would the sea give him his life back?

More to the point, was Andy giving him room for the soles of his feet?

* * *

Another dawn. On the wind-swept quay, the women waited for the fish auction to begin. Unlike the good-humoured banter which flashed back and forward between the tables by mid morning, there were only muted conversations.

Elsie flapped her arms to generate heat.

'You were a nurse, Mary. What were the VADs all about?'

Mary blinked. 'They were volunteer nurses, like me. Mostly middle-class girls, from colleges, or posh houses.'

'If they were posh, why did they want to be nurses?'

'They were mostly suffragettes, weren't they?' Aggie said, her cardigan sleeves pulled long over clenched fists.

'Suffragettes stopped fighting the government when the war started,' Mary replied. 'To show they were as patriotic as any man. As good as any man. Some of them volunteered to go out into the field and drive ambulances. Taking the same risks as the men. Earning the equal voting rights that they demanded.'

She checked the fresh rag strips on her fingers. 'There was a desperate need for nurses. More casualties than we had ever suffered before. There weren't enough doctors, surgeons and experienced nurses to go round.'

'Didn't one of these suffragettes throw herself in front of the King's horse?' an Irish gutter asked from the table below them. Gutting quines could hear a ha'penny drop at 200 yards, if there was gossip in it.

'That was an act of protest, wasn't it?' Aggie answered.

'More an act of madness. Who wants to vote in any case? Politicians are out for themselves. You can't trust them.'

The women stamped their booted feet. This early morning waiting time was always the coldest.

'Did you work at the front line?' Elsie asked.

'Only after I transferred into one of the Scottish Women's Hospitals field units. They were set up by Elsie Inglis — a brilliant surgeon, one of the first women to break into a closed male profession. She argued that the quicker surgeons could work on the wounded, the less the danger of infection. The War Office told her to go home and knit socks. So she set up her first volunteer unit, and the Belgians snapped up her offer of help. Then the French snapped up a second unit. And Elsie Inglis herself went over to Serbia, with another unit. They were taken prisoners of war by the Germans, then released. In 1917, when she was dying of cancer, she took a final unit out to the Eastern Front, to help the Serbs again, and brought her girls back through the Russian Revolution.'

'Quite a woman,' Aggie said.

'She knew her surgery. Her front line units achieved almost double the survival rates of big military hospitals. But you worked till you dropped, when there was a 'push' on. The longer you were there, the more experienced you became, the more responsibility you got. I finished up working in the theatre.'

In the distance, the auction bell rang.

'Thank goodness for that,' said Mary.

Within minutes, metal-rimmed wheels ground over the cobbles, as merchants' barrows brought up the fish they had bought. As always, with the oily herrings, degeneration was a problem. If the job wasn't done within the day, the fish were worthless. So gutters worked under constant pressure, filleting around fifty fish a minute, as fresh barrowloads spilled ceaselessly over the wide table tops.

Tired minds make mistakes. At the end of a long first week of the Orkney fishing, the girls were feeling the pace. A couple of tables away, a young Highland gutter's knife spun out of her hand. She grabbed at it, knocking it across her body.

The razor-sharp blade sliced deeply into her upper arm. Within seconds, there was blood everywhere.

Aggie and Mary heard the exclamations of the women round the other table.

'There's been an accident,' Aggie muttered.

Mary laid down her knife. She hesitated,

then pushed through the crowd of women, wiping her fish-slimed hands on the sleeves of her jersey to try and clean them. She and Gus Walker reached the young girl at the same time.

She was half lying on the ground, supported by her team.

'One of you lassies run for the doctor!' Gus called urgently. 'Quickly!'

Silence.

'There's no doctor on Papa Stronsay,' an English gutter said. 'The nearest doctor's down in Kirkwall.'

This wasn't one of Gus's teams, but that made no difference. Gutters and merchants were a tight-knit community, despite their competition. He was the only merchant here, and it was up to him to handle the crisis. Improvise.

He looked up. 'Mary. Can you help this quine?'

'My hands are dirty,' Mary said. But she knelt on the quay, and with gentle fingers pulled away the young girl's bloodstained hand. 'Give me a knife,' she demanded, and cut back the blood-sodden cardigan arm, clearing the wound.

It was long and deep. And pouring blood.

That had to be stopped. Mary looked into the girl's eyes. 'We've got to stop that bleeding,' she said gently.

Decision made, the calmness came. The detached concentration, born of five long years of nursing men with far worse wounds than this. Her fingers felt for, and found, the places where she must compress the arm to staunch the flow. She pressed gently, saw the flow ease, then pressed firmer still.

'Aggie!' she called over her shoulder.

'Here.'

'Go up to the hut. In my bag, there's darning needles. Take the smallest, and some white thread. Boil an inch of water in the kettle, and sterilize them. While you're waiting, get the iodine bottle and cotton wool from the medical cabinet.'

'Right!' Aggie started running.

'I'll go too,' said Elsie. She had overtaken the older woman long before they reached the hut.

Gus swallowed. 'What now?' he asked.

'Wait until the bleeding stops. Then stitch it up.'

All his instincts were to leave them to it. But he couldn't.

'What do you want me to do?' he asked.

His question was answered when the injured girl reached out a bloodied hand, and gripped his own fingers tight. He looked down at her: she was barely old enough to have left school. He was standing in for some dad who was out on a boat and fishing.

He found himself pressing back gently. 'We'll have you up and chasing the lads in no time, quine,' he murmured. 'Has the bleeding stopped?'

Mary glanced down. 'Nearly.'

All work had ceased, and the other women stood silently round. Then parted to let Aggie and Elsie through.

'We washed our hands,' panted Aggie. 'And Elsie's brought a wet towel, for you to use.' She held out the threaded needle, which she was holding carefully away from her fish-stained clothes. 'Here. Elsie's got the iodine.'

'Give me that first.' Mary wiped her hands, then poured some iodine onto a cotton swab. 'This will nip, lassie,' she warned. 'But we have to clean the wound, to make it heal.'

The youngster took a firmer grip on Gus's hand, and nodded dumbly.

Her body bucked, as the iodine bit.

'What now?' asked Gus, sweat cascading down his face.

'Give her something to bite,' Mary said, taking the needle. 'To stop her from shouting . . . '

'Bite what?' the Highland girl asked, with black humour. 'We've only got raw herrings here.'

'Take this.' An Englishwoman pulled off her apron, and hauled off her woollen cardigan. She rolled up a sleeve of the cardigan, and gently eased it into the wounded girl's mouth. 'Bite to your heart's content, my darling,' she said.

Mary took one deep breath, then another. Her racing heart slowed to a more regular beat. 'Catch her arm,' she ordered Aggie. 'Above, and below where I'm holding it. Now, hold her still . . . '

In her right hand, she took the threaded needle. In her left, with gentle fingers she drew together the edges of the wound. Blood seeped out, onto her fingers.

She ignored it. Frowning, she chose where the first suture should be made.

Then eased the needle in.

3

Gus Walker perched on a barrel, studying the sky.

'It's hot,' he said lugubriously. 'And what's worse, it's building up into thunder again. That isn't natural. Not for three days in a row, when one good storm should clear it up. And thunder's bad for fishing.'

His teams of women worked on stoically, lifting herrings from the table, gutting and grading them with a quick roll on both wrists, while his red-faced niece bent to take the gutted herrings and stack them neatly in layers in a new barrel.

'I said it was hot,' he repeated, to their busy backs.

'We heard you,' Aggie said. 'Now we're waiting to hear what you're going to do about it. You're the boss.'

'We're looking for leadership,' Mary said. 'Decisive action, to save us from heat-stroke and stop the fish from rotting.'

'It's the fish I'm worried about,' said Gus. He wriggled down from the barrel and came over to lift one, sniff it, then drop it back on the table.

'It smells nearly as bad as you,' said Aggie.

'At least it's got an excuse — it's dead,' Mary added.

Gus grinned. 'Less cheek,' he said. 'Is the dance still on at the weekend?'

Dances were impromptu events, on Papa Stronsay. Fisher crews drifted up to the girls' communal huts, bringing fiddles, maybe an accordion, or a simple mouth organ. Sooner or later, somebody would strike up, and the others join in — then the table and beds would be carried to the wooden walls of the hut, and the floor taken over for a dance and a ceilidh.

'Probably,' said Mary.

'If you're coming, I'm wearing clogs on my feet,' warned Aggie.

'I'm a fine dancer,' Gus protested. 'Always in demand.'

'Stick to playing a comb wrapped in paper,' Mary advised. 'Leave the floor to us bright young things.'

'What bright young things?' Gus looked around. 'Well, there's Elsie, I suppose . . . '

'I'm not dancing with you,' she said. 'I'm saving myself for younger men.'

'I'll tell your dad,' he warned. Then his attention wandered. 'Mhairi,' he called over. 'How's the arm? Healing properly?'

The young Highland gutter looked up from

her work. 'As good as new . . . see!' and she waved it above her head. 'Mary should set up as a seamstress — there's scarcely any sign of the cut.'

'That's more than I can say about the hand you gripped,' Gus replied. 'You left me with three broken fingers.'

'You've got seven left,' said Aggie.

'That's sympathy for you,' Gus mourned.

He frowned, and settled down again on his barrel. 'I came to speak to you both,' he said, more quietly. 'My quines will be moving down to Wick, with the boats. The fishing's poor. I'm thinking of resting a couple of teams and sending them down to Aberdeen early. It would mean some extra time off.'

Aggie turned quickly. 'At home in Buckie?'

'That's right. Instead of one week between the fishings, you'd have maybe three. Depending on how the shoals move, and where the boats are finding them.'

'I could spend more time with the bairn,' Aggie muttered.

'That's what I thought. That's why I wanted to speak to you first.'

'It would suit me fine.' Aggie turned to Mary. 'How about you?'

Mary hesitated. She herself was short of money. However, friendship was friendship. 'I'm happy to stay at home for a bit,' she said.

'And you, Elsie?' Aggie asked.

The young packer was engulfed in a wave of homesickness. Already she had been away from Buckie for five weeks. Too long. She wanted home.

'Suits me too,' she said.

'It's unanimous.' Aggie turned to Gus. 'Thanks. We'll do it.'

'I'm too soft-hearted. It will be the death of me.'

'We'll give you a good funeral,' Mary promised.

The cooper came over. 'Are you getting up from that barrel, or will I have to stamp you too?' he demanded of his boss.

'It would take more than a Crown stamp to cure him,' Aggie said darkly.

'Enough!' cried Gus. 'I'm away to practise my dancing.'

'That will put the fish down, faster than thunder,' Aggie sighed.

* * *

The glow of the ship's lantern sparkled like diamonds on the wet deck. But the crew of the *Endeavour* were too fed up to appreciate it. Cleaning debris from the last few yards of the mile-and-a-half-long net they had just hauled in with the steam winch, they were cursing steadily. Because the net was empty of herrings, and they would have to find another place and shoot the whole length again.

Johnnie Cameron rubbed his stinging hands. 'There's only one thing worse than rope burns — and that's jellyfish,' he complained. There was a mutter of agreement from the other seven deckhands.

Neil quietly coiled the last rope and its buoy, while the men watched Andy's silhouette in the deckhouse windows. Waiting on the skipper's call — what they did next, and where they steamed in their search for fish.

'I'll get some tea brewing,' he said.

The others scraped up the mess of jellyfish and seaweed, and shovelled the lot overboard into the black water. Herrings came to the surface in darkness, and the steam drifters were surface netters. So the men were used to working through the night. That didn't mean to say they enjoyed it — least of all when there were no fish to show for five hours' work. They knew without being told that the whole shift was about to be repeated. And might still bring about exactly the same result.

Neil hesitated, then opened the deckhouse door.

'I'm brewing tea. Want a mug?' he asked.

Andy stared moodily through black windows. 'It's the heat, and the thunder,' he grumbled. 'Drives the fish deep. Even if you're drifting right over their shoals, they can swim below your nets and you're none the wiser.'

Neil closed the door and leaned against it. 'The main shoals have gone east and south,' he said. 'We're searching for the stragglers.'

'Mmphm. Where would you try next?' Andy asked suddenly.

Neil was surprised: his brother must be at his wits' end to seek help. He stepped inside, opened the well-used sea chart in the lantern light, and put a finger on the jumble of depth soundings.

'We're here?' he said, as Andy nodded. 'Like you, I think the fish are running deep. But look sou'-sou'-west. Two hours' steaming away. There's a rising shelf and a reef. That should drive them up in the water. I'd shoot my nets there, on this side of the reef, across the tide.'

They studied the chart. 'It might just work,' said Andy. Being a skipper and expected to magic fish out of thin air was a burden more often than a pleasure. He straightened up. 'Tell the boys they can get their heads down for an hour or so, till we reach the mark. And bring a mug of tea to the deckhouse.'

'Right,' said Neil. Ten minutes later, he brought back a steaming mug.

'Thanks.' Andy accepted it, yawning.

'I'll take the wheel. What course?'

Andy hesitated. 'Steady as she goes . . . sou' by south-west,' he said. 'That's allowing for the tide.' He wedged himself in a corner, slurping hot tea. 'We need a catch,' he muttered. 'The prices are good, but we need a decent haul to get the benefit. It's been too up and down, this fishing . . . good one day, bad the next.'

He yawned again. He had been on his feet for hours — and it would be many hours yet before he got his chance to catch up on sleep. A skipper's life.

'Why not get your head down, with the lads?' suggested Neil. 'I'll take the watch, until we're nearer the mark.'

Andy frowned at him.

'Haven't had the shakes in days,' said Neil.

'You should be sleeping, with the rest of them.'

'I'm better awake,' Neil said quietly.

'Nightmares?'

Neil didn't reply.

Andy yawned again. 'Right,' he said. 'You have the wheel. I'll grab an hour's sleep.

You're doing fine,' he said grudgingly. It was clear that the comment cost him dear. 'A lot better than I thought. But nothing's changed.'

'I wouldn't expect it to change.'

Andy grunted and left the deckhouse.

Neil checked the course, bringing the wheel a little to port. The boat rose easily to the slight swell. He sensed, rather than heard, the creaming of the water breaking round its bows and sliding past the deck. It came back to him, the feeling that he was part of the boat, as much a part as its deckhouse, or the steam winch, or the old McKie and Baxter engine which pounded steadily. He could feel its beat through the soles of his boots. As if he had rolled back time.

The quiet noise surprised him. Then he pulled a face.

For the first time in years, he had found the urge to whistle.

* * *

Dawn comes early in the north. The crew waited, watching Neil coil the lead ropes for the net, as the steam winch chattered. The first sign that they were into fish was when gulls came swooping overhead and hovered, barely above the sea.

The winch slowed down, adjusting to its load. Padraig rubbed his hands: 'If there's stings, they'll be worth it this time,' he said.

As the net came in, it drew the first herrings over the side. With practised ease, the men flicked the net to dislodge the enmeshed fish. Leaping bars of silver, they slid around the crews' feet and slipped down into the main bunker in the hold.

The air around them was suddenly full of seagulls, wheeling and swooping, taking suicidal risks. It is a miracle how an empty stretch of sea, its sky broken by only a handful of gulls following the boat, can suddenly become a blizzard of white.

The weight of the half-full net drew the port side of the vessel low, and green water from the waves sluiced along the slanting deck boards. The men never noticed: in these northern waters, it usually did. You learned fast to stick like a limpet to the deck. Swaying against the boat's movement became such second nature that, after time at sea, it was dry land that moved beneath your feet.

There was little talk, just steady concentration on freeing the fish and stacking the heavy wet net — back-breaking work if you weren't hardened to it. As he bent over, stacking the net and its ropes, Neil felt a light punch on his arm.

He looked up. It was Andy, passing down the line of busy men.

Neil smiled, and settled to his work again.

* * *

The eightsome reel was going great guns, with laughter filling the wooden hut. The band — two accordions and three fiddles — were red-faced and perspiring. If this was their seasonal goodbye to Papa Stronsay, they were determined to finish on a high.

Mary stopped, panting, glad to have somehow survived Andy's last spin — wild enough to launch her into the harbour, if she missed her footing. He stood across from her, chest heaving, a devil-may-care sparkle in his eyes and his dark hair a-tumble over his brow. Elsie was right, she thought: he was a good-looking figure of a man, vital and confident.

'I'll have the next dance too,' he demanded.

'I'm already promised,' she lied.

'Then break your promise.'

'To my boss?'

'Then give me the next dance after that.'

'We'll see,' she replied.

The couples broke up, and headed back to their own groups, while the band gulped down their mugs of tea — no drink was allowed inside the hut. Mary saw Aggie coming towards her, real colour in her face.

'You've left your clogs at home,' she teased.

'I can run away faster from Gus without them.'

They slumped into wooden chairs, glad to catch their breath.

'You look great,' Mary said quietly. 'Just how you used to look.'

Aggie flushed. 'It must be the light — or the lack of it.'

Or the thought of going home, to see Tommy again, Mary guessed. She dabbed at her face with a handkerchief. 'I don't have another dance left in me,' she mourned. 'I'm out of practice.'

'That Andy — he's been chasing you all night. Elsie's fair jealous.'

'He can dance. He's light on his feet, and he leads well,' Mary admitted. She dabbed her face again. 'But I've had enough.'

The band confabbed, found another reel they could all play, then set their mugs aside and struck up again. Through the rush of men heading forward, Mary glimpsed Gus's determined face.

'My lie has caught up with me!' she exclaimed. 'I'm nipping out for a breath of fresh air.'

'What's up?' Aggie asked, as Gus closed in.

'Give me five minutes,' she pleaded. 'Let me get my clogs on.'

'No need,' he said. 'My mother was a Highland dance champion.'

'Aye, but your father was a coalman,' Aggie sighed.

Outside, the long summer evening was beautifully still. Mary drew in deep breaths of fresh island air, smelling of the sea, and seaweed. There was no urge to dance left in her: just a wish to savour the coolness and quiet. The sun was low in the sky — it barely went below the horizon at this time of year. She strolled down to the harbour, to watch it setting from there.

Away from the din of the dance, there was only the call of the seagulls and the gentle slap of ropes against masts from the boats moored in the harbour. She strolled past the scrubbed gutting tables, down to the edge of the quay.

A solitary figure hunched there. A man, absorbed in his work. Sitting on a rusting bollard, bent over something on his lap. A sheet of paper. As she quietly approached him, she saw there was a pencil in his hand, and he was sketching.

'Neil!' she exclaimed.

He looked up, with eyes that didn't see her.

'How do you draw sunlight, sparkling on

the water?' he asked intensely. 'In fact, how do you draw light at all?' Then he blinked. A slow smile lit his sombre face, as he stood up and hid the papers he had been working on behind him.

'Mary Cowie,' he said quietly. 'Wearing the sunset like a crown.'

Mary felt her face redden. 'What were you doing?' she asked.

'Nothing,' he shrugged.

'You were sketching,' she said. 'Can I see what you've drawn? Please?'

'It's rubbish. Beginner's stuff.'

'Let me judge that.' She reached gently behind him, drawing out the papers he had been working on. A school exercise book. She opened it at random, in the light from the dying sun. Seagulls: standing, flying. Herring gulls, young gulls in immature plumage.

'Why, these are beautiful,' she said, turning the pages.

Men's faces, caught sleeping. A tangle of ropes and nets, drawing across the stern. Then a series of sketches of the harbour scene he had been working on. A rough outline of ships and quays: three separate attempts to sketch in waves and light. She could sense his growing exasperation.

'Where did you learn to draw?' she asked.

'In the convalescent hospital. A doctor

there got me started — he said it might help me to find my mind again.'

'And has it?'

His eyes looked directly into hers. Grey and green, like the sea, she thought.

'Sometimes.' He teased the book from her fingers. 'I've never tried to draw light before. I don't know where to start. You can't just leave the reflected light as white bits in the water . . . that gives no sense of movement, of *life*. Maybe, if I bought a book on art, it would teach me how to draw — how to catch the light.'

'You don't need a book,' she said. 'What you've got already is something nobody could ever teach.'

He shook his head. 'Just outlines. A bit of shading. There has to be more to drawing than that.' He glanced up. 'Are you going on to Wick, with the others?'

'No. Back to Buckie. Gus has enough teams in Wick. He's giving us a couple of weeks off, then we'll start again, down in Aberdeen.'

He nodded. 'We're going to Buckie too. The boiler's acting up, and Padraig says we need to get an engineer to help him put it right. Maybe Gus will send you down with us?'

'If it saves him train fares, we're as good as on your ship already,' Mary declared.

* * *

The small, muddy car drew alongside them, and its window slid down. 'Well, 'home is the sailor, home from the sea',' quoted Jonathon.

''And the hunter home from the hill',' Mary completed the quotation.

'Jonathon!' Aggie's face lit up, as she swung the kitbag from her shoulder to the ground. 'So you haven't been struck off yet?'

'No — but the Medical Council are getting closer,' he smiled. Then turned to Mary: 'So you know the Robert Louis Stevenson poem?'

'I do,' said Mary, grimly. It was one that she'd read many times, to the blind in the convalescent hospital. A favourite, with the power to silence and console men whose lives had been torn apart by the war.

Jonathon's sharp ear picked up the nuance. He waited, but she didn't elaborate. 'Where's the young girl?' he asked Aggie.

'Elsie? She'll be home already.'

'And you're walking back to Nether Buckie?'

'I feel more like running. I feel so bad about my bairn,' Aggie said.

'Hop in. I'll drive you home. I'm out on my round of visits, and I'm passing through there anyway.'

Mary squeezed into the back seat, wedged

in by the kitbags that held the two girls' belongings: they were shifting camp, like soldiers. She looked up to see the doctor's blue eyes, smiling over his shoulder.

'Has Gus done his usual trick, sending you down cheap, in one of the local fishing boats?' he asked.

'We came back in the *Endeavour*. They're here for repairs,' said Aggie. 'All his other teams are in Wick. But we're home for a fortnight, then off again to Aberdeen.' She was itching to see her boy's face, watch his surprise when she came in. Aberdeen was in the future: and she would worry about that later.

'*Endeavour*? That's the Findlays' boat?' asked Jonathon.

'It is. Andy had his crew waiting on us, hand and foot.'

'He's a good lad,' said Jonathon. 'How's Neil?'

Mary waited. 'Better, I think,' she said, when Aggie didn't reply. 'Life at sea suits him. And he's taken up drawing — he's pretty good.'

Jonathon grunted: someone in the convalescent hospital must have been up to date in his reading of medical journals, where rehabilitation was an emerging and experimental field.

'How are you getting on yourself?' Aggie asked. 'Still living on carrots?'

'Just about,' he grinned ruefully. 'To tell you the truth, I've been run off my feet. My best nurse has just left, to go south and marry a serviceman. I have one local girl, to cover the whole cottage hospital. We're struggling to cope.' He drew up, in a squeal of brakes. 'Here you are,' he said. 'I shall waive my tip.'

'You can wave goodbye to the fare, as well,' said Aggie. She opened the car door, stepped out, then looked back. 'I'm scared,' she said in a small voice. 'What if wee Tommy doesn't recognize me?'

'He will,' Jonathon reassured. 'Nobody else in town has a face like that . . . '

Aggie laughed. 'I'll get even with you,' she promised.

Behind her, the cottage door opened. Chrissie, her mum, stood there: round her skirts a small face peeped. The boy's eyes opened wide. Then he was hurtling down to leap at his mum, all arms and legs. Aggie caught him and swung him high, round and round at the full stretch of her arms. He squealed.

'I better go,' said Jonathon. 'If he sees this car, he'll be into it in a flash — you're sitting in his seat, by the way. Where can I drop you off?'

'I'm fine,' said Mary. 'I'll get a cup of tea, then walk home. Thanks for the lift.'

'Pleasure.' Jonathon half rose to help as she hauled out the two kitbags, then sank back. No help was needed. Expertly, she hoisted one onto her shoulder and gripped the other by its straps. He watched her slim figure walk towards the cottage: more than able to look after herself, like all these local quines. She turned and smiled back at him. He waved, then let his clutch in.

An attractive young woman, he thought, as he headed away.

Down in the harbour, there were other comings and goings. Andy hesitated at the foot of the ladder. 'Are you sure you don't fancy having a pint with the boys?' he asked. 'It will still be on credit, until we get our wages from the fishing.'

Most of the town lived on credit, during a fishing: the fishermen's wives having every loaf of bread and box of matches meticulously entered in the grocery's black book, on the understanding that as soon as their man was paid, the debt would be settled. It always was: bad credit meant that a family might have to starve until the wages came from the next fishing — which could be eight or ten weeks away.

'No. I'm cleaning out the galley. I'll be

home later,' Neil said.

'Suit yourself.' Andy trotted after his crew, who had already worked up a fair head of steam as they set course for the Harbour Inn.

Neil worked on steadily. Now that they had finished the trip, he could wash out everything properly in fresh water — every drop of which was precious for drinking and cooking at sea. So fresh water was rationed. You washed out the galley in water drawn in a bucket from the sea: and you washed your plates and pots and pans in condensed steam from the engine. Even the crew had to wash in cold seawater. There was an art to filling a bucket while the ship was in motion. Get the timing wrong, and you risked being pulled into the sea — or having the cost of a bucket and a rope deducted from your wages.

'You're busy.'

Neil turned round, to see his father leaning against the galley doorway.

'And you're blocking my light,' he smiled.

Eric came over, gripped his son's shoulder briefly. 'How are ye feeling?'

'A lot better. You were right about the sea.'

'I was right about you.'

Eric felt for his tobacco tin, and went through the ritual of taking a flake, then rubbing it between the heels of his hands, to crumble it. He glanced up. 'How was the fishing?' he asked.

'Good, and bad. Andy's got the figures in the Catches book.'

'But you covered your costs?'

'At a rough guess, yes. Andy keeps the figures to himself.'

'Skipper's work,' said Eric absently. 'How is he shaping up?'

'He's good. With a bit of coaching, he could be better than either of us. You hung up your boots too soon, Da. You could have brought him on.'

'I'm too old, too slow,' said Eric. 'He did nothing stupid then?'

'He did as well as he could, in a poor fishing.'

'He's too hot-headed. Takes too many risks.'

'He's trying too hard. That's all,' Neil defended him.

'Aye,' said Eric. Doubtfully. He puffed at his pipe. 'Right. I could swallow a pint. Are you coming?'

'I've just turned down Andy and the boys.'

'Does that mean you're turning me down as well?'

'I didn't say that.'

'Then what's keeping you? Let's go.'

* * *

Jonathon looked down with a mixture of sympathy and irritation at the nurse's crumpled body on the floor. He had a severely injured, possibly dying man on his hands in the cottage hospital. The last thing he needed right now was a fainting nurse. But he could understand why she'd reacted like that: this was the worst emergency he'd handled in years, and he was fighting panic himself. Even doctors are human.

Sympathy aside, there were priorities: fainting came a distant second to someone bleeding to death. He reached across her, in the small theatre, taking the injured man's pulse as he lay deep in shock. Desperately weak. No time to mess about. If only the fellow's workmates had stayed to help, instead of bolting. They could have carried her out for him: cleared the way. Jonathon bent down, turned the young nurse over onto her back and took a firm grip underneath the shoulders.

The cottage hospital doorbell rang. Typical. Whoever it was would have to wait. His priority was to get the nurse out of theatre, then start on a radical surgical procedure, which he hadn't attempted since his student days. Entirely on his own.

As he struggled to haul the nurse out, he heard footsteps break into a run along the hallway.

'Wait a minute. I'll take her legs.'

A young woman brushed past him, gripped the nurse's ankles, and helped him lift her from the floor.

'Down here will do,' he gasped, laying the body down gently in the corridor, then turning her onto her side. She would have to lie there until she recovered — or his more seriously injured patient died.

He looked up. 'Mary Cowie!' he exclaimed.

'I heard down the town that there had been a bad accident. I knew you were short-staffed, from what you said to Aggie. I've done theatre work. I rushed up to see if I could help.'

'God sent you,' he replied. 'It's going to be an amputation — have you tackled any of these?'

'More than I want to remember. What happened? Where do we scrub up?'

He guided her to the sluices and turned the taps on. 'Shipyard worker,' he summarized, concentrating on building a lather between his fingers. 'Was working a steam winch. They were hauling a fishing boat up onto the slip. The winch jammed . . . ' He held his hands up under the running water, carefully sluicing off the last traces of soap. 'The man stopped the engine and went in to find out what had caused the problem . . . the brake slipped . . . the ship started sliding back into the harbour . . . and the poor devil got drawn into his own machine. Its gears have eaten most of his right arm.'

'Morphine?'

'Enough to sedate — but he was far into shock. Didn't want to use too much.'

They went into the theatre, where the mutilated body lay under the sharp white lights. Jonathon checked again. Pulse weaker still. Blood starting to run thin, almost like dirty water. This was the worst emergency he had tackled since he left Glasgow and came back home.

He was conscious of Mary quietly checking the tray of surgical instruments, adding a few more vascular clamps. Then he saw her upend a phial and draw morphine into the syringe. With well-practised ease. The reprimand died in his throat: a theatre nurse from a war hospital would be more experienced than himself.

'How much?' he asked.

'Just what we always used.'

He glanced at the side of the syringe, nodded. Then fixed on his mask.

'Not enough bone left to mend,' he said quietly. 'I'm taking off what's left of the arm . . . maybe here . . . '

'Leaving a pad of muscle, when you close the wound?'

'Exactly.' He looked up. 'Maybe we're too late. He has very little blood left and has already suffered horrendous shock — before we even start.'

'He'll live,' she said. 'I've seen men recover from worse than this.'

'It's ironic,' he said. 'But you've had more experience of radical surgery than the man who is doing the operation.'

'We'll manage fine,' she reassured, her voice muffled by the mask.

'Let's hope you're right,' said Jonathon.

He hesitated. The surgical saw glinted from the tray, his fear of using it drawing his eyes back to it every time. He suppressed his fear. Forced himself to concentrate, to think. How far above the remnants of shattered bone should he cut?

The only way to know was to expose it.

'Scalpel,' he said.

And felt the instrument being slapped firmly into his gloved hand.

* * *

They washed together at the sluice. Jonathon's legs were trembling from his reaction to the strain of working methodically through an amputation. He had never, not in all his life, felt so exhausted.

'Did your war surgeons use blood transfusions?' he asked.

'Routinely, in the last year of the war. When we could get the blood stocks.'

'Did it really reduce the effect of the trauma and surgical shock?'

'Dramatically. Have you any blood stocks here?' Mary asked.

Jonathon shook his head. 'No call for them. And, outside war surgery, the whole concept of transfusions is still in the research stage.'

'We can analyse his blood type. If it's common, ask his mates to let us check their blood. If we can match two or three, it would be enough.' Mary dried her hands.

Jonathon studied her. 'It's asking the impossible but, do you know . . . ?'

'Yes. The unit's surgeons taught us how to analyse and match the groups.'

'Could you . . . ?'

'Have you a microscope? Glass plates?'

'I'll get them.' He turned at the door. 'Miss Cowie,' he said.

'Mary.'

'Mary. Between the two of us — and the credit is fifty/fifty — we have just about saved the life and what's left of a destroyed limb for that young man. Before I thank you, I have a simple question to ask . . . '

'Fire away,' said Mary, her mind on the

analysis she was about to do.

He stared at her, serious blue eyes in a dark and sombre face.

'Someone with your skills is wasted as a gutting quine. Would you come and work for me as my senior nurse, in the cottage hospital? I need you. The whole town of Buckie needs you. What do you say? Will you be our nurse?'

4

Mary stared at Jonathon. Returning to nursing had never crossed her mind. After her voluntary work at the convalescent hospital had finished, all she'd wanted to do was get back home. Return to normality, find a decent man, and settle down. The war had claimed enough of her life already.

'I mean it,' Jonathon said quietly. 'You are exactly what this town needs. A nurse who can act as a theatre sister, in emergencies.'

'But I was a volunteer. I don't have proper nursing qualifications.'

'You've learned from experience, working in that front line unit. Nurses aren't like doctors, spending years studying before practising. They're trained more by their matrons, by hands-on working with patients than by teachers. You handled that amputation as competently as any experienced theatre sister. I couldn't have managed without you.'

Mary flushed. 'I only came here in case you needed help,' she said.

'And I did. You have no idea how much. Say yes. Please?'

'But I can't,' said Mary. 'I've given my word to Gus Walker. I'm under contract to work for him until the season ends, in Yarmouth.'

'Maybe, if I spoke to him . . . ?'

This was spiralling out of control. Mary shook her head.

'I can't,' she repeated. 'It wouldn't be fair to Gus — or the other two girls in my team. Gus would never be able to replace me, this late in the season. It would leave him short-handed and cost the other two their jobs.'

'But I desperately need an experienced nurse.'

His insistence was driven by real need, not a whim, Mary judged.

'All right,' she said. 'I'll work for you, until we leave for Aberdeen. That's two or three weeks away — giving you time to look for someone else.'

'You'll be paid, of course,' Jonathon said.

His blue eyes were earnest, in a face which responsibility had moulded into a severity that was at odds with the verbal sparring matches which Aggie's presence always sparked. Then, it was his impish good humour she had seen.

'Let's get on with analysing the blood groups,' Mary said.

After four hours, they had found two matches with the injured man's workmates, and given him a blood transfusion that would set him on the way to recovery. Tired, but elated, Mary knocked on Chrissie's door.

'Where on earth have you been?' the older woman asked. 'We were expecting you hours ago . . . '

'There was an accident in the harbour. I've been helping Jonathon.'

'Oh,' said Chrissie. This was a different Mary from the one who had come back from war, she thought. The dark shadows and drawn look had gone: in their place a sunburned face, and eyes with a sparkle in them, a new confidence. What had happened up at the cottage hospital?

'Aggie is playing with the Wee Man,' she said.

They went through the narrow hall to the main room at the back, where Aggie and her son were sprawled on the carpet, playing with a new-looking wooden steam train. 'She's never been on her hind legs in two days,' Chrissie smiled. 'I told her it was daft to buy the toy, when our money was so scarce.'

Aggie sat back on her heels. 'Where have you been?' she demanded.

'Giving Jonathon a hand. Nursing an emergency.'

'I thought you were done with all that?'
'So did I.'
Aggie pushed herself from the floor. 'I'll get the kettle on,' she said. 'How was Jonathon anyway?'
'He did fine. It was a really bad accident. But he handled it well.'
'He would,' Aggie said proudly. 'He's the best there is — but don't tell him.'
Mary went through to the kitchen with her friend. 'He wants me to come and be his nurse,' she said. 'At the cottage hospital.'
The hand which was lifting a spoonful of tea leaves into the pot stopped: then completed the action. 'Oh,' said Aggie. 'And what did you say?'
Mary didn't notice. 'I told him we were under contract to Gus.'
'And?'
'I said I'd help, until we left for Aberdeen.'
'And?'
'That's it.' Mary looked searchingly at her friend. 'What's up?'
Aggie rubbed the small of her back, with a hand that trembled. 'It's my back,' she said. 'I've been hunkered down with wee Tommy for longer than was good for me.' She poured three cups of tea. Added milk, and sugars.
'Once you've had that cup of tea, you can

be Tommy's stationmaster,' she said. 'And, if you thought that nursing was hard work . . . '

⋆ ⋆ ⋆

The boat felt dead in harbour, Neil thought. Of course there was movement, from the swell that surged across the harbour entrance, and noises from the mooring ropes rubbing against the quay. But the *Endeavour* always seemed to be waiting for someone to bring both her and her old engine back to life.

He stayed quiet, at the far end of the table in the crew's quarters. Sure, this was a skippers' meeting, past and present. Which included him, from the years before he left to go to war. Yet somehow, he felt an interloper: his dad and young Andy were the main skippers, to his mind. Covering the past, the present, and the future. He was here on sufferance. He sipped his tea.

Eric studied the Catches record that Andy had kept on the Orkney fishing, slowly turning the pages as his mind converted the figures into the hard cash that was needed to keep the boat afloat. Finally he sighed, closed the book and pushed it back to Andy.

'Aye,' he said. 'It could have been worse.'

'We did as well as anybody else,' Andy replied indignantly. 'The fishing was poor.

Ask any of the boys, when they come back from Wick.'

'No need,' said Eric. 'You've told me.' He gulped a mouthful of tea, then began to search through his pockets.

'The tobacco's in your right jacket pocket,' Andy exploded. 'Your pipe is in your breast pocket. And your matches have been in the left jacket pocket since I was a bairn at school. It's never changed — so why the performance?'

'Mmmphm,' Eric said absently. He continued searching, then brought out his tobacco tin and eased a dark flake away from the rest of the block inside. Slowly, deliberately, he began to grind it between the heels of his hands.

Andy looked across at Neil, impatience verging on anger in his eyes.

'We've had three thin years,' Eric mused, ramming the tobacco into his pipe, and beginning the search for matches. 'That's two years more than outside investors are happy to suffer. But it's the same for everybody. Until this year, most of the boats were laid up, or crewed by men as old as myself.' He stopped, sparked a match, held it over the bowl of his pipe, then puffed steadily, filling the cabin with acrid smoke.

He fanned the burnt-out match in the air,

killing its flame. 'This is the first year we've been able to fish where we wanted, with proper crews. Now that the U-boats are gone and our lads are back from the war.'

Andy scowled at the scrubbed table top. The war was a sore point: at first too young to enlist with the others, then held on a tight rein aboard the *Endeavour* by his father, exempt from military service because he was in an essential industry for a desperate nation's food supplies. In a boatload of old men, he had grown up quickly, doing more than his share.

But he hadn't been to war. Neil and the others had.

White feathers were never fashionable in Buckie. They were a silly, fatal game played by safe and opinionated middle-class ladies down south. There was more than enough risk at sea, and not a woman in the north who didn't know that.

'We more than covered our costs on the Orkney fishing,' Andy argued.

Wreathed in tobacco smoke, Eric nodded. 'You've done that, and more,' he agreed. 'If we keep that going down the east coast, there will be money to share out among the shareholders. But, only enough to cover this season. Not enough to compensate for the last three seasons.'

Ownership of most fishing boats lay in the hands of a limited number of shareholders. The skipper usually held a share, although he was paid the same wages as his deckhands: the family held a few shares — all three men at the table were shareholders. But the problem was that where shares were held by one or more local businessmen, they were looked on as an investment, and had to make a return like any other financial asset. Worst of all, if the bank held shares, then they kept a cold commercial eye on things.

Over a long, lean spell, outside businessmen tended to sell on their shares: if the family couldn't buy them back, then the bank might step in and buy another share, or several other shares. Each new purchase giving it a stronger voice in the running of the ship. Until it effectively owned it, and could sell it to recoup the debt.

Eric took another gulp of tea. 'When Donald Christie offered us his two shares last year, we couldn't afford them. So the bank stepped in, and took over his investment.'

'How many shares do they hold now?' Neil asked. Thinking that it should be himself who was carrying the worry of finances, not his father.

'Five.' Eric's answer was clipped.

Neil pulled a face. The family held seven between them.

'We can always buy them back,' argued Andy.

Eric stared at him. 'With what?' he asked. 'Unless you bring up a treasure chest in your nets, we can only pay a dividend. That's why it's so important we have a good season. We have to make a big enough surplus to get them off our backs.'

'If the other boats are no better off, then there's a limit to what the banks can do,' Neil argued. 'They won't force you to sell the *Endeavour*.'

'Some of the boys coming back from the war might fancy having a go at being skippers. Then borrow the money to buy their boat,' said Eric. 'That's always been the way, in the fishing industry. New lads take a gamble on themselves. While the banks are glad to sell boats that aren't making money.'

He stood up, abruptly. 'We have to keep costs to a minimum. If repair work can be postponed until next year, then it will be. We must make a good surplus this season. Buy time. Worry about the cost of the repairs next year.'

'The work on the boiler had to be done,' exploded Andy.

Eric nodded. 'Therefore it was. When are

you putting out to sea again?'

Andy frowned. 'We need to stock up with provisions, load coal, water, all the usual stuff. Day after tomorrow.'

'Where are you heading?'

'We've missed the Wick fishing,' said Andy. 'Better to head east and south, and work off Fraserburgh and Aberdeen for a bit. Get south of the shoals. Be waiting for them, not chasing after them, like we were in Orkney.'

Eric nodded. 'That's what I'd do, myself.' He pushed the empty mug towards Neil, a twinkle in his eye. 'Here's some dishes for you to wash,' he said.

Neil grinned. 'My fingernails have never been so clean,' he said.

The old skipper headed out, sniffing the harbour air. 'Weather's going to break,' he judged.

'It's all one to us,' said Andy. He left his empty mug on the table. 'I think I'll take a turn through the town. See if I can find Mary Cowie. Take her out for tea at the hotel.'

'Bring her home, and save your money,' Eric advised. 'You've been doing a fair bit of chasing after that Cowie quine?'

Andy shrugged. 'God put women on earth for men to chase,' he said. Then climbed limberly up the rusting hoops of the quay ladder.

Eric watched him go. 'Will he ever settle down?' he sighed.

'He could do worse than Mary Cowie,' Neil said quietly.

Eric's pipe had gone out. He took it from his mouth and stared at it. Then his shrewd blue eyes looked up from under iron-grey eyebrows. 'What about you, my loon?' he asked quietly. 'When will you find a quine, and settle down?' After Chrissie had raised the idea, he'd found that it wouldn't go away.

'Me?' Neil snorted. 'The mess I'm in, what woman would have me now?'

Eric started searching for his matches again.

'That's for you to wonder, and her to say,' he replied mildly.

* * *

'Are you sure you can't come with me?' Andy demanded.

'Absolutely,' Mary replied. 'I've been working all morning at the cottage hospital. Aggie and me are heading back there now.'

'What's up?' he asked. 'Has an epidemic broken out?'

'Not yet' said Mary. A touch grimly.

'Andy shrugged. Ah well,' he said. 'One

woman's misfortune is another's good fortune.' He smiled at Elsie, who was visiting Chrissie. 'Can you drink tea with your pinky up in the air?' he asked.

'Indeed I can,' she answered calmly.

Although her heart was beating all over the place.

'Then come on,' Andy ordered, rather than invited. 'I'll treat you to scones and tea at the hotel.'

'Listen to him!' said Aggie. 'Buckie's answer to Andrew Carnegie . . . '

'You're just jealous I asked Elsie first.'

'More like relieved,' Aggie replied.

Andy grinned: he had a good sense of humour. With women, anyway.

They watched the young couple stride off towards the town. 'They look the part,' observed Mary. 'But he'll lead her a merry dance. Are you ready then?'

'Just about,' said Aggie. 'Wait till I kiss the Wee Man goodbye.'

They trudged up towards the cottage hospital. The sky was full of racing high grey clouds, the westerly wind blustery. Mary breathed deeply and contentedly: it was these wild, wind-torn skies that she had missed down south.

'What does Jonathon say about this?' Aggie asked suddenly.

'About you coming?'

'About us scrubbing out his hospital.'

'He doesn't know.' Mary had only decided this morning that she could suffer the dust and cobwebs no longer. Things had been neglected: none of the matrons she had worked for would have tolerated it. Dirt in the wards, or the theatre, was an infection waiting to happen.

When she'd challenged the young nurse, the woman had bristled: the place was swept out twice a week. Not good enough, Mary thought. Even if dealing with the problem herself was going to make an enemy for life, she could live with that.

They reached the cottage hospital, and Mary went in through the back door to the kitchen. With Aggie hesitant behind her, she searched the cupboards for pails and scrubbing brushes. There were pails to spare, but only one good scrubbing brush — the other looked as if it had been used by Mrs Noah, after the flood.

'I'd be better with the mop,' Aggie judged.

'If you mop the floors, I'll take the scrubbing brush and do the corners. And the surfaces and the beds need a wipe-down with disinfectant in the water.'

Aggie rolled up her sleeves. 'Where do we start?' she asked.

'In the theatre.' Mary saw Aggie's face. 'Relax, there's nobody in it.'

'What about the man who was hurt in the boatyard?'

'He's through in the men's ward. I changed his dressing today. He's coming along fine — he was trying to learn how to play cards one-handed when I saw him last.' Mary frowned. Operating tables and equipment would be threatening to anyone who hadn't worked with them on a daily basis. Plus it was crucial that these should be absolutely sterile. Therefore better if she did them herself.

'You do the floor of the theatre, and I'll do the rest,' she decided.

It took an hour of solid work. Then they moved into the main women's ward, where only two beds were occupied. They pushed the other beds into the middle of the floor, and Aggie volunteered to make a cup of tea for the invalids, while Mary started scrubbing.

She was blowing hair away from her hot face, when Jonathon came in.

A startled silence, when he saw her on hands and knees.

'What are you doing down there?' he demanded.

'Giving the place a proper clean-out,' she replied. 'The first step in good nursing. When did your last nurse leave?'

'Six weeks ago.'

'It looks like it.'

Jonathon coloured. He'd been meaning to chivvy the young nurse into doing a better job. Then, in the pressure of work, he had forgotten. The other nurse had made sure the place was spotless for him. He'd never had to think of it before.

Aggie came in with a tray of teacups.

'Typical!' she snorted. 'Make a cup of tea, and men come out of hiding.'

'You too!' he exclaimed. 'What are you doing here?'

'Clearing up the mess you've made,' she said. 'Mary brought me here to help her. I'm her apprentice.'

'And you're starting by making tea?'

'We've all got to start somewhere.'

'Then where's my cup?'

She made a great pretence of checking a list. 'I don't have your order,' she said. 'But I see your name down here for the washing up.'

'That's all I'm fit for,' he mourned. 'Where's Julie?'

'Through in the men's ward,' said Mary over her shoulder, working away.

'I'll go and get her,' Jonathon said.

Aggie sighed. 'So that's two more cups of tea?'

'Just one,' he replied quietly. 'I want her to see what she should be doing — then down on her hands and knees, and doing it too. If she's going to learn the job of nursing, how better than by working with experts?'

'Am I included as an expert?' Aggie asked hopefully.

'I'll tell you once I've tasted your tea,' he said.

* * *

For once, the northern sun shone from a cloudless sky, and a shimmering heat haze danced over Buckie. Jonathon was setting out for Strathlene, all windows open in his tiny car to create a much-needed breeze.

At the far end of town, he saw a young woman walking along the dusty road, with a tiny child in tow. Aggie. Slowing down, he stopped alongside.

'Where are you walking to this time?' he asked.

'Wee Tommy was restless. I'm taking him to the beach.'

'At Strathlene?'

She nodded.

Only a shingle and boulder beach, he thought. He could do better than that

— repay her for the work she had done at the hospital.

'Hop in,' he said. The words were only half out his mouth, when the child had bolted into the back seat.

'The wee devil,' sighed Aggie. 'I thought I had him in a proper grip.' She opened the door. 'You're getting him far too used to travelling in comfort.'

'Boys love anything mechanical,' he said. 'In my day, it was steam trains.'

'I thought it was Roman chariots,' she teased.

'Oh, them too,' he laughed.

'Where are you heading?' she asked.

'To see a patient. I'm quiet, today. So, how about me taking the rest of the afternoon off, and going for a run to Cullen? A proper sandy beach for Tommy to play on?'

'I couldn't possibly,' Aggie demurred.

'Why not? If he gets stung by a jellyfish or nipped by a crab, you have your own physician waiting. What more could you ask?'

Not much, thought Aggie. 'But my mother's expecting me back . . . ' she said.

'Not for hours, if you were walking to Strathlene. I'll drive you home, in good time. What do *you* say to it, Tommy?'

'Yes!' The little boy bounced up and down in the back seat.

'Yes, please,' reprimanded his mother.

'You're outvoted, two to one,' laughed Jonathon.

'Why do men always stick together?' lamented Aggie.

It was the start of a near-perfect afternoon. They waited for twenty minutes while Jonathon visited his patient, then drove through Findochty and Portknockie, the two fishing villages on the road to Cullen. There, he parked the car underneath the railway viaduct, and they turned Tommy loose on the sandy beach.

The small boy ran, tumbled, got up covered in sand and ran again. Was into the water before his mother could swoop down on him and take off socks and shoes: but these dried in her hands as they walked along.

'I've never really played at the shore,' she sighed. 'The sea always meant work for me. From collecting mussels to baiting my father's longlines, when I got home from school, to following the herring as a gutter quine after that. We never had time to play . . . Look at him, dragging that dead seaweed through the edges of the waves. He'll be soaking wet, when we get him back the car.'

The sun was warm on their backs. They sat down, watching the child.

She turned, smiling. 'You're teaching me to be idle, Jonathon.'

'You're giving me an excuse to hide from my patients,' he said. 'I'm enjoying this break as much as you — which is half as much as he's doing.' He took out his pocket watch. 'Let's give him another half hour. Then we can go up to the Cullen Hotel for a pot of tea.'

'I'm not dressed for it,' Aggie protested. 'Besides, he'll leave a trail of seawater and sand.'

'It's a holiday town,' he laughed. 'They're used to it.'

Later, in the hotel, they sat sipping tea. The cake stand the waitress had placed in front of them had been emptied. Two cakes for Tommy, two for Jonathon to encourage the child, and one for herself — until she decided to make it two all round. It wasn't a day for half measures, Aggie decided.

She glanced around the posh tearoom. They looked just like any other family in the place, she thought. It was a thought which made her unreasonably happy.

'It's been a perfect day,' she said.

Jonathon shrugged. 'Look on it as wages-in-kind,' he said. 'A thank you, for all the work you and Mary did in cleaning the hospital. More tea?'

She shook her head. Jonathon poured himself another cup.

'She's quite a girl, that Mary Cowie of yours,' he said cheerfully.

Aggie's smile froze.

'It's not often you get all these qualities in a woman,' he continued. 'Obvious intelligence, ability to make her own decisions — and a wealth of nursing experience which both the town and myself could use.'

He sipped his tea. 'You should have seen her, during that amputation. So calm, so much in control. Watching the patient, anticipating whatever I needed — steering me like one of her famous lady surgeons would have done. I drew on her strength. I owe her a huge debt of thanks.'

'Mary's one of the best,' Aggie said. Her voice dead.

'She's absolutely wasted as a gutter quine — no offence, Aggie.'

'None taken.'

But there was. His unthinking comment left a deep and silent hurt.

Jonathon checked his pocket watch. 'Well, we had better be getting back, or your mother will be wondering where you are,' he said.

They drove home in silence, the child asleep in the back, Aggie retreating deep into herself, and Jonathon relaxed and happy as he drove home.

'We must do that again,' he said, when he dropped them off, and lifted the sleeping child onto his mother's shoulder.

'Thanks. It was a wonderful day,' said Aggie. Forcing a smile.

There was something in that smile or the tone of her voice which made him stare, puzzled, after her.

Aggie brushed past her mother. 'I'll put the bairn to bed,' she said. Fighting back tears that wanted to come, no matter how she suppressed them.

Chrissie stood in the doorway, waving goodbye to Jonathon. Then turned, frowning down the empty hallway. All her instincts on red alert: something had happened. Something which had hurt her daughter deeply. It couldn't be Jonathon — he would never hurt Aggie. They had been friends from childhood: thick as thieves. The two of them had scarcely ever fallen out.

Unless. Chrissie's mind leapt to a possibility, a conclusion.

She sighed. That would never happen. Firstly, Jonathon came from a totally different world to the one they lived in. Secondly, and worse, she suspected that her lonely daughter had just discovered the widow's curse. The thing that happens when, no matter how young you are, or how bonny, the man looks past you and sees the child at your skirts. Then, often without even realizing it, feels unable to clear the final hurdle. The one which involves taking into his own name a child which another man has fathered.

'I'll put the kettle on,' she called up the stairs. To silence.

* * *

Mary shivered. They were waiting for the morning train to Aberdeen, and a cold haar from the sea was drifting over the station platform.

'This is worse than Orkney,' Elsie said. Putting a brave face on things, trying to block out of her mind that she was leaving home for four or five weeks.

Aggie said nothing. Mary had never known her so quiet. Was it worry about leaving young Tommy behind?

'We'll soon be back,' she encouraged. 'Aberdeen's the nearest place we'll ever work. You can nip back for a weekend, if you can beg a lift.'

'Can we do that?' Elsie asked eagerly.

'If you're lucky. Sometimes a crew steams home to their families on Saturday, then heads back to Aberdeen over Sunday night.'

'I wonder if Andy will do that?' Elsie said.

'Don't throw yourself at him,' warned Mary.

'Don't throw yourself at any man,' Aggie said darkly.

It was the first time she had spoken. Mary looked at her, surprised.

Through the mist streaming past the station building, they heard a car door slam. Someone else catching the early train. Jonathon came through the station doors, rubbing his hands.

'Good,' he said. 'I was scared I'd missed you.'

'Are you going to Aberdeen too?' Mary asked.

'Too busy for day trips. I came to see you off, and thank you for the work you've done at the hospital. I don't know how we'll cope, with you away.' He turned to Aggie. 'Nobody has insulted me for two whole weeks. Where have you been?'

She shrugged. 'Busy.'

'Was Tommy any the worse for his soaking in the sea?'

'He was fine.'

'A great day that,' said Jonathon.

But his eyes and voice were troubled. Something had gone badly wrong. He sensed it but, like most men, had no idea of what he'd done to cause it. Therefore he didn't know what to say, to put it right. He hated this awkwardness. For the first time ever, there was an invisible barrier between himself and Aggie.

He sighed. Then focussed on what he had come to say.

'Mary. I know you're under contract until December. But you'll still be home between the fishings. If you can, I'd like you to drop in to help us when you're back in Buckie. That job is yours for the taking. I'm seriously thinking of keeping it open for you, until January.'

'Thanks,' Mary said awkwardly. 'I'm happy to help, when I can.'

In the mist beyond the station, a steam engine whistled.

'Here's your train,' said Jonathon. 'Need a hand with your luggage?'

'We'll manage fine,' said Mary.

The engine steamed out of the mist and ground to a halt at the small station platform. With most of its passengers likely to be picked up nearer Aberdeen, the three girls had it to themselves. Despite their refusal, Jonathon heaved their kitbags, one by one, into their compartment.

As Aggie passed him, he caught her elbow gently.

'What's wrong, quine?' he asked quietly.

He used the word with affection: she heard it as a job, in which other people were wasted. 'Nothing,' she answered, snatching her elbow away.

'Safe trip!' he called from the platform, as the wheels of the engine spun, and the carriage eased slowly through the clouds of steam.

'What a nice man,' Elsie said.

Mary was staring at Aggie. While Aggie looked out at fields she couldn't see for haar. And a blur of tears.

Something was wrong. And it involved Jonathon. A misunderstanding? Had Aggie found herself falling for him, and drawn back? She knew that Aggie was nowhere near as tough as she seemed. Behind the ready banter, she was vulnerable: still in an emotional turmoil, adjusting to the death of her husband, and the need to work and leave her child behind.

She squeezed Aggie's work-roughened hand. Whatever it is, I am your friend and I am here for you, that squeeze was meant to say. There was no answer.

Mary stared out of the carriage window at different shades of grey. Here a tree, there a cow, loomed out of the mist and disappeared. Visibility so poor, she couldn't see the edges of the fields, let alone the sea,

It would be there: it always was.

Her attention turned inward. Something had changed in her over the last two weeks. In early summer, she had travelled this line in the opposite direction trying to put as many miles as possible between herself and nursing. Wanting nothing more than to get home and pick up the threads of the life she had known before.

She was a fisherman's daughter, and had thought that was enough.

It wasn't. Not even close. To her surprise, she had loved every minute of the last two weeks. Nursing, organizing, helping Jonathon with the more serious cases that he handled in the cottage hospital. She had felt useful: even fulfilled. Satisfied with every day's work she put into the place.

There was more to life than being a gutter quine.

She looked blindly out of the carriage window. Was Jonathon right? Did her real calling lie in being a nurse again?

5

With the *Endeavour* gone, the busy harbour seemed empty. Eric dragged an old fish crate to a sheltered corner of the harbour wall: there was an edge to the wind, which spoke of the northern autumn coming. From this wooden throne, he could keep an eye on both sea-bound traffic and the bustling quays beneath the town.

Despite being retired for a year, he hated being left behind. Even if it was by his own choice, because he'd had his day, and now it was up to his sons to make a living from the sea. He reached into his pocket for his tobacco tin.

On the wall behind him, a young seagull was mewling — chased away by its mother and left until hunger forced it to fend for itself. The sound of birds had filled every day of Eric's life. He barely heard them yet was so attuned to the noise they made that, if it varied, he instantly checked for a reason. As he would for a change in the beat of the engine which had driven his boat.

Like any skipper, he had watched for gulls hovering above the sea, to tell him where the fish were shoaling. Now, even seagulls were struggling in their search for herring. He crumbled the tobacco in his hand, then filled his pipe. This was starting to feel like the seven lean years in Egypt, he thought wryly. The whole town, not just its fishermen, were discovering what it was like to tighten their belts.

His pipe unlit, he rested his hand on his knee. There was a rhythm to life — years of plenty, and the years between. For as long as there had been fishing, it was always thus. You learned to put savings to the side when there was cash to spare: just as you helped others out who were less fortunate than yourself. Widows of fishermen long dead but not forgotten. Or men too old, or ill, to make their own living from the sea. The fishing community made sure that no one was neglected, or went hungry. You looked after each other. It was a way of life.

Eric scrubbed his free hand across his chin. This was changing; he could sense it. The war had stolen a generation of young men, and sent home restless women who had done men's work in the cities, and were reluctant to go back to the role they had always known.

Once you see life's alternatives, it can give you itchy feet. For himself, the sea and his family had been enough: he had never bothered to search out alternatives. But the war had forced change — and it wasn't finished yet. Would the sea heal, then hold, men like Neil? Would the Mary Cowies of the world make a home, settle down to raising a family? Renewing the old place?

Or would too many drift back to the brighter and easier life they had seen, taking away the very people on whom the future of Buckie rested?

What if the herring went too? Once he had thought there were fish in the sea for everyone. Now, he was less sure. Had the war against U-boats destroyed fishing stocks? Had the shoals simply swum elsewhere? Or had he and his kind already emptied the sea, as they tried to keep their boats out of debt, and their families in clothes?

Eric stirred restlessly on the wooden crate, not liking where his thoughts were taking him. If the lean years continued, and the herring stocks failed, then not even those who wanted to stay would find enough work to keep them. What then of his beloved community, and its way of life?

It was the young who would leave, to find work. Taking away themselves, and their children — both born, and still to be born. The community would get older and greyer: less able to look after its own frail and struggling members. A town of old men and women. While the seagulls called and the waves crashed in spray against the harbour, as they had always done.

'A penny for your thoughts.'

He looked up. It was Chrissie, with Aggie's little lad in tow.

'A penny? They're not worth even half of that,' he muttered.

'They were deep enough to make you forget your pipe.'

'Aye,' Eric said. His hand went straight to his left pocket for his box of matches. 'Will things ever get back to how they were, Chrissie? Will the town get back to what it was before the war? Will Andy and Neil ever settle down, and bring up their families here? Like you and me once did. Or is it all going to change?'

'Michtie me!' she said wryly. 'These are black thoughts for any man.'

He struck his match, held it over the bowl of his pipe, and puffed. 'Aye, but it's happening, isn't it? Everything we knew is under threat. If the fishing industry dies, there's not a store in town that doesn't live on ships' orders for ropes, and coal, and provisions. And there's not another shop in town that doesn't draw its living from the families of the lads out fishing. If fishing goes, what will happen to the town? To folk, looking after weaker folk, as they did before us and as we do now? Can you tell me that, Chrissie?'

She studied him. There's a danger, when you have known someone all your life, that you see him as he was in his prime. Not as he is. But Eric was still a fit and able man. Having left the sea to make way for his sons, rather than because he couldn't cope with it any more. Now restless in his new-found idleness. A man who had stopped working too soon.

'Of course everything's changing, Eric,' she said. 'Nothing stands still. If it did, we would all turn into stone.'

'Is it changing for the better?'

'The young think it is. It's only old folk like us who look back to the past.'

'Mmphm.' He took the pipe from his mouth. It had gone out again. Almost as if he had lost the heart to puff at it.

Chrissie read his mind. 'It's a poultice you're needing to put on the back of your neck, to draw that pipe,' she scolded. 'But I have the very cure for you.'

'What's that?' he asked.

'Come back, and I'll make you a cup of tea,' she said. 'Have you had your breakfast yet?'

Eric shook his head. 'No, I forgot. I came down to help the loons cast off.'

'Well, there you are!' she said triumphantly. 'I never knew a man yet who could talk sense on an empty stomach.'

* * *

'It's my turn to clean the hut and cook,' Aggie said.

'I'll help,' Mary offered.

'No need. Go up to the town with the others. It's the weekend.'

All of this without eye contact. This was not the Aggie she had known and worked with for years. Something was badly wrong, but Mary was unsure how to tackle it. Clearly, her company wasn't wanted — but there were other priorities. Like trying to get to the bottom of Aggie's problem, and put things right.

She picked up the brush, and began to sweep the floor.

'I can do that!' Aggie said crossly. 'I told you, it's my turn.'

'I heard you.'

Mary kept on sweeping. She felt her friend's irritation rise, then ebb. Now. If there was a time to strike, this was it.

She stopped working. 'What's up, Aggie?

What's the problem between us?'

'Nothing's up. There isn't a problem.'

Aggie banged the dirty pots and pans around, as she cleared the area round the well-chipped kitchen sink.

'These last three days, you've scarcely said a word.'

'You're imagining things.'

The dirty pots took another beating.

'Even Gus has asked what's wrong.' Mary turned, to see Aggie leaning on closed fists at the kitchen sink, her head bowed. Quietly, she set the brush aside, then walked over to her friend.

Aggie turned her face away.

'You're the best friend I've got,' said Mary. 'What's wrong?'

Aggie blindly shook her head.

'There must be something.' Gently, Mary pulled her friend round. Aggie's face was wet with tears. 'Oh, Aggie! Tell me what's wrong.'

Somehow, they had their arms round each other, Aggie's shoulders shaking like a child who thinks the whole world has turned against her. Mary held her tight, until the sobbing eased. Then Aggie pushed her away, but gently.

'It's my own fault,' she said, her voice choked.

'What is?'

'A widow woman — thinking about another man. I feel guilty . . . I feel angry . . . I don't know what I feel.'

'What other man? And why not? You have your whole life in front of you . . . you're young, yet. You can't just lock yourself away. Tom wouldn't have wanted you to do that.'

'It's just . . . ' Aggie started. 'He's been so good with wee Tommy. So patient, so easy with him.'

Jonathon! Who else? Mary had guessed right when she sensed that something had gone wrong between the two of them at the railway station.

'I took a friendship,' Aggie said. 'And tried to turn it into something else . . . something it was never meant to be. I got ahead of myself, that's all. Now I've probably messed up everything.'

'With Jonathon? Never. I doubt he even knows what's gone on.'

Aggie shook her head. 'Not him,' she said. 'He's too decent a man. It was all me. Adding two and two and getting twenty-five.'

Mary frowned. 'Why not Jonathon?' she demanded. 'The two of you have been as thick as thieves for years.'

Aggie stared at her. Let silence build.

'Well, you have,' Mary said, defiantly.

'Maybe,' said Aggie. 'But now, all he can

talk about is you. 'Mary did this, Mary said that, Mary dropped in and saved the world . . . ''

Mary stood stricken. 'But I didn't know,' she finally said. 'All I was trying to do was help him out when he was short of a nurse. When he offered me the job, I was as surprised as you.'

Wind moaned round the corners and found the cracks in the ancient wooden hut. Cracks which other quines in other years had stuffed with newspapers, now stained and faded into unreadable print.

'So that's what was wrong?' Mary asked quietly.

Aggie nodded.

Mary reached out and took a firm grasp of her friend. 'But, Aggie. I don't want your Jonathon. Right now, I don't want any man. I'm in as big an emotional mess as you. I don't know what to do with my life. I don't know whether I want to stay here and settle down. Or go back to nursing. I'm so confused.'

Aggie screwed up her handkerchief into a tiny, sodden ball, her eyes on the floor. They came slowly up to meet Mary's.

Mary shook her gently. 'Whatever happens, I don't want to lose our friendship.' Then she blinked. 'I know. When we get back home, why don't you come up to the hospital with me? Help out with the nursing work. I'll show you how to make the beds, lift the patients. Most of nursing is only doing what you do already with wee Tommy. Common sense. Being a mother to everybody.'

'I couldn't,' Aggie started.

'Why not?'

'The Wee Man. The only time I've got with him is when we're in Buckie.'

'Then work part time. Look, if you want to show Jonathon that you can do more than hold a gutting knife, here's your chance. He's desperately short of nurses. I can teach you within days to be a better nurse than the lazy lump he has there. What do you say? Are you willing to try?'

A glint came back into Aggie's reddened eyes. 'And you can show me?'

'Like other nurses once showed me.'

Aggie pushed her away. 'Right, quine,' she said. 'Get on with that sweeping. I'll run the pots and dishes through. If we put our backs into it, we can nip up and have a look at the Union Street shops, before I start the dinner. Come on!'

'It's a deal,' said Mary, reaching for the brush.

* * *

The paraffin lantern swung on its hook, and the ship's timbers creaked. The net had been shot and the crew were grabbing some sleep before hauling it. The engine was silent, only the small stern sail working, giving the ship enough steerage way to control the rate and direction of her drift.

Neil hunched over the school jotter, his pencil busy. Sketching Andy's face, relaxed in sleep. The burden of command had already etched some lines on it, and there was a small frown beneath the tumble of dark hair over his brow.

The brown rat appeared silently and suddenly on the table top. These fishing boats were full of vermin, no matter how many the crews caught and killed. With all the fish guts scattered and rotting around the harbours, docklands were Rat City and their inhabitants adept at climbing mooring ropes and colonizing boats.

The rat's nose twitched, its beady eyes on Neil. The nose assessing the half-eaten sandwich on the table. No mathematician could have done a quicker or more accurate sum on the balance of risk.

Neil saw the beast from the corner of his eye. Watched quietly, and with a touch of humour. The rat eased towards the sandwich, flowing smoothly and silently in the shadows cast by the lantern above. It reached its goal, and paused, checking again. Neil kept up the steady scratching of his pencil.

The rat sniffed the bread, then the uneaten cheese which filled it. It looked sharply at Neil, ready to flee at the slightest movement. Rat and man watched each other stealthily. The rat put its paws on the edge of protruding cheese, and began to nibble.

As Neil began to sketch, on a corner of his page. Barely moving his eyes to take in his subject, which was making inroads into the cheese, while watching him throughout. It was Neil's sandwich. Left lying there because he wasn't hungry, and dared not go to sleep. He was glad to see it find a properly appreciative home.

On the page, the rat's head and shoulders emerged, the almost human tiny hands. The whole image vibrating with the electric tension of the real rat.

His pencil scratched on. Live, and let live, Neil thought. Out in the trenches, he had got used to the rats running over his sleeping — or sleepless — face. This, in the quiet creaking and gentle movement of the boat, was better.

Infinitely better.

* * *

Mary smiled. He was sitting on a rusting bollard in the harbour, head tilted back, watching white clouds scamper across the sky. Wondering how to draw them and show their movement, she was prepared to bet.

'Are bollards all you can afford?' she asked his back.

'Mary Cowie,' he said, and there was a smile in his voice. He spun on the bollard and rose smoothly to his feet. 'I would know that voice anywhere.'

The sea had tanned his face, she thought. Given him back his confidence.

'You were watching the sky,' she accused, 'and wondering how to draw these clouds with the sun behind them.'

'Guilty as charged. Why aren't you up in the town, laughing at the new Chaplin film with the other quines?'

'I didn't feel much like laughing,' Mary said.

The good-humoured grey-green eyes sharpened. For a second, she felt they were looking deep inside her. She shivered, turning her head away, to stare over the forest of masts, where half the drifters in the world were moored. Only Yarmouth would have more boats in harbour.

'When did you leave Peterhead?' she asked.

'We got here this morning. You have a

problem that's bothering you?'

His directness should have disconcerted her. It didn't.

'I have,' she admitted.

'Something you thought was settled, and is anything but?'

She stared at him. 'Is it that obvious?'

He smiled. 'It wasn't hard to guess. All the ones who went to war are restless. The homes they were wearying to see again turned out to be nothing like they remembered. The jobs that were theirs, for life, felt more like a cage. Because, for each and every one of them, they brought their war back in their hearts.'

'That's about it,' Mary admitted frankly.

'You're not alone; there are thousands like you. You're no longer the schoolgirl who gutted herrings and hadn't a care in the world. She's gone. Now you are a woman, who has seen things and done things which have changed your life forever. Turned you into a square peg. Is that what it feels like, now?'

Mary didn't answer.

'The whole town was full of how you went into the hospital and helped the doctor with the worst emergency we've seen in years — taking over when young Elspeth fainted.' The steady eyes, so like the colour of the sea, crinkled. 'I'm guessing that, when you left the war, you thought your nursing days were over — and now, you aren't sure.'

Mary sighed. 'What did you say earlier about guilty as charged?'

'So, are you going back to nursing?'

Strange how she could talk openly to this man, when she was walking on thin ice with Aggie. It was almost a relief to air the problem. 'I can't think straight,' she said. 'The more I try to make up my mind, the worse I go round in circles.'

'Go on. I'm listening.'

'When I came north, all I wanted to do was reach home and live like a normal person. Stop seeing people with horrendous injuries. Stop trying to cheer up men who will never do another day's work in their life — not even selling matches at the street corner, because they have been left without arms or legs.'

'We were a pretty disgusting-looking bunch,' he agreed quietly.

'You were still humans! With your hopes and plans destroyed! I felt so much pain for you. Wanted to magic you better, but there was no book to tell me how . . . '

'Because there *is* no magic cure for war,' he said. 'Our power to kill and maim people grew faster than our skill at sticking them together again. For German lads, as well as us.'

'I know,' she said. 'I nursed them too.'

He studied her quietly. 'War scarred you. Left you wanting nothing more than to crawl home, get your job back from Gus. Settle down one day, and raise a family.'

Mary shrugged. 'I just want to be normal.'

'But you're not normal, Mary Cowie. You stand head and shoulders above the normal. The war has made, as well as destroyed you. It has taught you how to help people through dark nights. Give courage back to men who are afraid. To hold their hands, and cry for them. Stand in for the mother, the wife, the girlfriend, the sister they had left behind — who is too scared to see them now. It taught you to be the vital difference in people's lives. To be a nurse, where others are afraid.'

'How do you know all this?' she demanded.

'Because I was there. I was one of them. Not in your hospital, but in one exactly like it.'

Mary had a strange sense of being totally equal, almost at one, with this man. No barrier between them. 'There's something else,' she said. 'Something that a man could never understand.'

'Try me.'

She fought to gather her thoughts: to make the clearest possible sense.

'In these Scottish Women's Hospitals, there was more at stake than nursing dying men. We nurses felt we were helping other women who were braver than ourselves. The ones who were pioneering being women doctors in a profession that was exclusively male. Breaking down the barriers. Proving that women doctors and surgeons were every bit as good. Almost fighting a war, behind the war. A war that's still going on today . . . will go on for years.'

'I know. It was an Elsie Inglis hospital that channelled me to convalescence. They were doctors first, and warriors for their cause second.'

Mary laughed. 'Most of them would put it the other way round.'

'I was being polite.' There was wry humour in his voice.

'Jonathon's offered me the chance to be his nurse,' she blurted out.

'And you're taking it? After the herring season?'

'I don't know. My head's spinning. I can't decide.'

He nodded. 'Have you ever climbed a mountain?'

'There's not many mountains near Buckie.'

'You'd be surprised,' he said. 'There's a trick to it. I discovered it while I was healing, and found mountains I had to climb inside my head. When you start out, don't look at the summit. That way you trip and fall. Take it one step at a time, and watch where you're putting your feet.'

'I don't follow you,' Mary said.

'Help your doctor friend out. Stop fretting. Take it a day at a time, and see how you feel, when the season ends. By December, the decision may make itself.'

'And if it doesn't?' Mary asked.

'Follow your heart, not your head,' he said simply. 'Because your head will always find twenty different reasons for not doing something that scares you.'

Mary had never met a man to whom she could talk so freely. Someone who listened, and understood. Saw her more clearly than she saw herself.

She turned away. 'You're a dangerous man, Neil Findlay. You see straight into a person's soul . . . then hold up a mirror.'

He watched her go, then called: 'Mary Cowie?'

She turned. 'Yes?'

'While I'm holding your mirror, think about this. Why just be a nurse? It takes brains and courage to be a woman doctor. You have both to spare. Why not train to join these women warriors of yours? Be a pioneer, fighting for women's place in the medical profession?'

She stared at him. 'Me?' she said. 'Never!'

'Why not?'

The sea-green eyes were level, steady.

She couldn't answer him.

* * *

The news reached the gutting tables, long before Gus came to tell his teams. It passed like a ripple of water through the hundreds of quines on the quays of what was one of the biggest and busiest fishing harbours. A disaster touching everyone, but hitting hardest the teams from Buckie.

All work stopped, and the Buckie quines clustered round Gus when he plodded up, his head drooping. 'So, ye've heard?' he asked bleakly.

A murmur of agreement. Duncan Farquhar was well known, the youngest son of one of the main fishing families in the town.

'What happened, Gus?' Aggie asked.

He shrugged. 'It was black night, now that we're in August. Nobody knows what happened — or when. Maybe a wave took him from the deck . . . maybe his feet got caught in a rope, or the net they were shooting. One minute he was there, doing his job. The next time they looked, he had gone.'

'Didn't they turn back and search?' one of the other women asked. Knowing that the worst time to fall overboard was when the boat was shooting net, and miles of rope and net stretched behind the stern, waiting to foul the propeller and leave the ship drifting helplessly.

'They did a wide sweep,' Gus said. 'Then they put the stern lifeboat into the water. Half the crew rowed back and forwards where they'd been, while the other half hauled the net in. There was no trace of him.'

'So, when did they find the body?' Mary asked quietly.

'An hour after dawn. They must have passed him a dozen times, in the dark.'

There was a heavy silence. Behind them, you could have heard a pin drop, as the other women listened. Accident and death were no strangers to any fishing community. That didn't stop it from hurting, when it happened.

Gus scuffed his feet on the quay. 'The loon had two brothers on that boat . . . ' he said, then couldn't speak.

Aggie patted his back. 'There now,' she said. Tears in her own eyes.

Mary scrubbed her face with the sleeve of a fish-stained jersey. 'What are the Buckie men doing?' she asked.

'Going home. To wait for the boy's funeral.' Gus shrugged. 'I knew the boy. I know his family. I'd like to be there myself . . . but . . . '

'But what?' asked Aggie.

'There's you quines to think about. If I'm not here to buy, then there's no fish to gut. And wages lost, when I pay you at the end of the fishing.' The girls were paid for the total fish gutted, cured and packed, over each fishing. It had always been so: no work, no pay. Everything pivoting on the amount of herring landed.

Aggie planted her hands on her hips. 'Well, I knew the loon, and his family too,' she said fiercely.

'And me,' said Mary. 'We want to go to the funeral, just like the men.'

'Duncan was my half-cousin,' Elsie said, in a small voice.

'That's right. On your father's side,' Gus said. These old families were so interlinked through marriage that it wasn't easy to keep track.

'We're *all* going back,' another Buckie woman declared, to a murmur of general agreement. 'We want to be there, to support his family.'

Gus blew out his cheeks. 'I knew you would, my quines,' he said, with pride in his voice. 'But I couldn't ask you. Right, we finish tonight. Those of you who can, get a lift from the boats going back. The rest of you . . . I'll pay half your rail fare home.' He paused. These women were giving up wages, to pay their respects. His heart ahead of his head, he added: 'No, I'll pay your train fares home myself.'

He winced. 'Just nobody travel first class, that's all.'

His weak joke for once didn't draw a single smile.

Nobody felt like smiling.

Elsie tugged at Mary's arm. 'I'll be right back,' she said.

'Where are you going?' asked Mary.

Elsie was halfway down to the boats already. 'I'm going to see if Andy will take us home,' she shouted over her shoulder.

* * *

'Mmmm. Yes. I suppose so,' Jonathon said absently. Frowning as he studied the case notes in his hand.

'That means either he doesn't know, or he wasn't listening,' Aggie translated.

'What?' Jonathon's head came up, and he laughed. 'Sorry,' he said. 'What were you asking, Mary?'

'Where did you learn to sniff a diabetic's breath?'

'Experience — no, the first time I heard it was from an old doctor I worked with in the Glasgow slums. The apple-sweet smell, he told me. 'That's the surest way of knowing you have a diabetic on your hands, boy'.'

'He called you 'boy'?' asked Aggie. 'When was this? A hundred years ago?'

'No. It was when we were chiselling out the Hippocratic oath on stone.'

'You should have had better things to do, than carve out a swearie word,' Aggie scolded. She handed over some letters and small packages. 'Here's your post.'

'Thanks.' Jonathon glanced at the case notes again. 'The temperature is coming down nicely, the pulse rate's entering normal range. We keep up the treatment, I think. Plenty fluids . . . it doesn't matter if she doesn't feel like eating. If she does, only something light.'

'Right,' Mary said. She turned to Aggie. 'Now that she's recovering, I'll show you how to give a bed bath. That's a simple way of making her feel better.'

Jonathon turned away, idly flicking through the mail. He'd deal with it later, after the Farquhar boy's funeral. He lifted out a crisp, white envelope with its neatly typed address.

More official-looking than the rest. He hesitated, then laid down the others and eased open the envelope's flap.

A lawyer's firm, from Inverness? What were they wanting?

His frown deepening, he skimmed through the first paragraph. Then stopped: went back and read it again, slowly. Then a third time, shaking his head, as he finished the rest of the letter.

'What's up?' Aggie asked.

'Johnnie Meldrum is dead.'

'Who?'

'The man who gave us the cottage hospital — or at least this building, to be used as a cottage hospital.'

'And?' Aggie asked blankly.

'This is from the legal firm winding up his estate. The heirs to the estate have instructed them to sell the property — it looks as if they're wanting cash.'

'Sell our hospital?' Mary asked.

He nodded, too shocked to think clearly.

'But they can't do that! Not if the man himself gave it to you. There must be a contract, somewhere?'

'That's just it,' said Jonathon. 'The house was gifted for the benefit of the community, and the deal was sealed with a simple handshake. Like you and your fishing contracts, Johnnie's word was his bond.'

'But he must have left some instruction?'

'No mention of that here. I'm wondering if he never got round to it. He was always such a fit and busy man — death might have caught him out. He probably thought it would be years before he needed to write his will.'

'But, something so important . . . ' Aggie protested.

'I can ask them to check,' Jonathon said. 'But I have a feeling that the only man who could confirm the gift is no longer with us. And I don't know where that leaves us — unless it's without a leg to stand on.' He stared at them. 'He *must* have made a note of it, somewhere . . . told his bank, his lawyer.'

Aggie shook her head. 'What will happen to the town, without the hospital?'

'I'm going to Inverness, to see them,' Jonathon decided.

'What if he didn't leave a note?' Mary asked.

'The property will be sold from under us,' Jonathon said heavily. 'They have given us until the 3rd of January. Then that's exactly what they intend to do.'

6

'What sort of people would steal a cottage hospital?' exclaimed Chrissie. 'Does anybody want another scone?' She fussed round the small group who had gathered in her house after the funeral service, blessing the impulse which had prompted her to bake that morning.

Jonathon tried to wave her away, but found another scone had somehow transferred itself to his plate. 'In fairness, they're not stealing,' he said. 'It looks as if Johnnie Meldrum died before he got round to changing his will. That's all.'

'But surely, if somebody explained this to the lawyers?' Aggie said.

He nodded. 'I'm going to see the senior partner. Talk through our position.'

He hesitated, then picked up the scone and began to spread it. Most days, he had no idea where his next meal was coming from — or when. So he'd grown used to taking food where he found it.

Eric grimaced. 'We can't afford to lose our hospital. It would leave Banff or Elgin as the nearest place with one.'

'If thc heirs want cash, the only way we can keep the hospital is to buy it from them,' Mary said. 'We might have to negotiate a price . . . then raise funds to buy it.'

'Where would we ever get that kind of money?' Chrissie demanded.

'They'll want a king's ransom — a big house, in its own grounds,' Eric grunted.

'Maybe if we explain how important the hospital is to the community, they'll ask for less than the full price,' Jonathon suggested.

'Would other landowners be able to help?' Mary asked.

'By giving us another property? It took years to convert the one we have.'

'I was thinking more about donating money. Nobody's going to come up with the full amount. But if we could raise some money from local landowners, then more from businessmen in the town, maybe even the bank, then the townsfolk . . . if everybody gives something, it could all add up.'

'Forget the bank,' Eric said grimly. 'And most fishermen have barely enough to live on. Which means that local businesses are suffering too. This couldn't have happened at a worse time.'

Jonathon pushed aside his empty plate. 'We've got to do something,' he said determinedly. 'We can't just sit and let it happen.'

'Oh, we'll fight,' growled Eric. 'If we lose that hospital, while the fishing's bad . . . it could mean the end of Buckie as we know it. So we fight, as if our lives depend on it.'

'We need to use our heads,' Mary warned. 'Not go off at half-cock. First, we must find out where we stand. Next, what courses of action are open to us. Then decide which looks the best.'

'The only way to know where we stand is to ask people,' Aggie said. 'Why don't we split up, each of us seeing different people? Then report back?'

'Good idea,' Jonathon said. 'I'll handle the lawyers. If Aggie and Mary rope in Gus, he might sound out the other businessmen in the town. And if Eric and Chrissie talk to as many townsfolk as they can reach. Just taking the temperature of the water, at this stage. Exploring the support we can expect, and looking for bright suggestions.'

'There's still the landowners,' Mary said.

Aggie looked at Jonathon. 'You're the only one of us who can talk posh.'

'Not that posh,' Jonathon said. 'But, if it comes to buying the place ourselves, then I'll do it. It would be better if I took a couple of others, like Eric and Gus.'

‘Gus slurps tea from his saucer,’ Aggie cautioned.

‘I doubt they’ll be serving us tea,’ Jonathon answered grimly. He stood up, looking around the table. ‘We’ll start as this small group. But if it turns out as I expect, then we’re going to have to call the town together. Because this is going to affect each and every one of them.’

* * *

A few days later, Jonathon found them, with Eric plucking a silver threepenny bit out of the child’s ear, down in a sheltered corner of the harbour.

‘His granny can’t be washing them,’ Eric complained.

‘His granny was doing fine — until some daftie started that trick,’ Chrissie said.

Eric’s shrewd eyes studied Jonathon. ‘Well, did you see the lawyers?’

‘I did,’ said Jonathon. ‘It’s as bad as we feared. They’re sympathetic, say the promised gift was entirely in keeping with the man they knew. But they can only go on their documentation and Johnnie never formalized the gift. I don’t doubt for a second that he truly meant to — but he died before he got round to it.’

'That's what I expected,' Eric sighed. 'But I hoped for the best.'

'On my way home, I dropped into a couple of local landowners,' Jonathon continued. 'They were sympathetic, but said they had neither money nor property to spare. Maybe I should have waited for you and Gus . . . '

'It would have made no difference,' Eric said. 'In any case, Gus is in Aberdeen by now, maybe even Eyemouth. He was keen to take his teams there quickly, and let them make up the wages that they'd lost.'

He grimaced. 'You're not the only one to bring back bad news. I spoke to the harbour businesses. They're willing to help — but at best they can spare only a few pounds. Then I spoke to the bank about us maybe having a committee, and getting a loan from them. The manager had me through the door before I finished the sentence.'

'Where does that leave us?' Chrissie asked bleakly.

'I honestly don't know,' Jonathon replied, his heavy heart reflected in the words. 'Have you spoken to the local lads?' he asked Eric.

'They're with us — but have only pennies.' Eric began to search through his pockets for tobacco. 'We're going bottom-up,' he growled. 'We can dip into our hip pockets and help each other out — but whose hip pocket is big enough to buy back the hospital?'

'You said we'd fight!' accused Chrissie.

'Oh, we will,' he reassured. 'But we'll have to find something other than money to throw at them.'

There was a bleak silence, broken by the distant clamour of gulls.

'Mind you, I have still other landowners to visit,' Jonathon said. 'But don't hold your breath. Landowners, for generations, have hung on like bulldogs to whatever land they had.'

Eric lit a match, staring at it absently until it burned his fingers. 'We'll think of something,' he said, hurriedly waving out the flame. 'They're not going to walk away with our hospital. Not without a fight.'

Defiance wasn't enough, thought Jonathon. They needed a new plan. He wished with all his heart that Mary and Aggie were here to offer ideas. Two bonny women with brains to match their looks. He stopped. Aggie was his friend: he had never thought of her before as bonny. Yet she was. From nowhere, he saw a curl of dark hair against her neck. He fought to clear his mind, be sensible.

'If only . . . ' he said.

'Aye,' said Chrissie. 'The girls. We're missing their enthusiasm and their energy. Their courage. They're young, and the world belongs to them — to make, or mend. Old folk like Eric and me, we only see its problems.'

Eric took the unlit pipe out of his mouth, as if to speak.

Then put it back, and began his search for matches.

* * *

This sheltered corner of Eyemouth harbour was Buckie-in-exile. Elsie smiled at the thought. The five of them had drawn up fish crates and sat in an easy circle, chatting. After ten days working here, she liked Eyemouth best in the fishings. It was the first time she had ever seen a harbour stretching up the banks of a river running through the town. Where the narrow streets, with their haphazard collection of tall houses and shops, kept the worst of the cold wind from the gutting tables.

She smiled across the group to Andy: he winked back.

'So they're finding it harder than they thought, back home?' Neil mused.

'Jonathon's letter says they've raised plenty of goodwill — but no money. So where we go from there, to buy the hospital, I don't know.'

'We can't just give up,' said Aggie.

Andy perched on his crate: he had a fit man's sense of discomfort at the thought of hospitals. 'Something will turn up,' he said. 'It always does.'

'But what? And from where?' Mary demanded. He shrugged.

'Has Jonathon spoken to the landowners yet?' Neil asked.

'Yes, but they didn't want to know.'

Neil frowned at his booted feet. 'The Johnnies-come-lately, maybe.'

'Who?' Aggie asked.

'Maybe these were the small lordlings whose families stole crumbs of land from bigger tables. These will hang into every inch of ground they've got. Maybe Jonathon should try the Seafields, the biggest landowners in the north?'

'Don't they come from Cullen?' Mary asked.

'Maybe, but their lands stretch right up along the coast.'

'I'll mention them. And he was asking when we'll be coming home — he wants a town meeting, before we leave for Yarmouth.'

'You'll be home in a couple of weeks. A month here is normal.'

Andy stood up. Restless by nature, he knew they were putting out to sea in the early dusk. Time was precious, and was being wasted. He glanced across at Elsie. 'Fancy a cup of tea, up the town?' he asked. She was a pretty quine, and would fill the time in nicely.

Elsie was on her feet in a flash. Aggie gently pulled her down again.

'What's the fishing been like?' she asked sweetly.

Andy shrugged. 'We've caught our share.'

'Then you can treat her to a fruit scone as well?'

Andy stared, then grinned. 'If she pays half. Or bakes it herself.'

'Listen to him! There's more than small lordlings that are tight with their money!' Aggie laughed. 'And him halfway to making his first million pounds. I've said it before — Andy is Buckie's answer to Andrew Carnegie . . . '

She stopped. 'That's it!' she whispered.

'What is?' Mary asked.

'Forget the Seafields,' Aggie said intensely. 'They're only rich because they sewed up their pockets centuries ago. Who is the richest man in the world? Andrew Carnegie, in America. And he's a Scotsman. Why don't we write, and ask him to help us buy back our hospital? He's always building new libraries and things. If anyone has money to spare, and is in the habit of giving . . . it's him.'

Once stated, the truth was obvious. But there was a flaw.

'Isn't Carnegie dead?' asked Mary. 'I think he died last year.'

'Rats!' said Aggie.

'Didn't a foundation take over all his charity work?' Neil muttered.

'Then write to that,' said Aggie. She gripped Mary's wrist. 'Write back to Jonathon. Tell him to get in touch with Dunfermline. They've just built a big library there — maybe they'll know how to reach this foundation.'

Mary absently rubbed her wrist. 'I've a better idea,' she said.

'What's that?' demanded Aggie.

'*You* write to Jonathon, and tell him,' Mary said gently. 'The idea is yours — so why don't you tell him yourself?'

* * *

Daylight had almost gone, and the lights of the fishing fleet along the quays were growing brighter by the minute.

'Will they really help us?' asked Mary.

'The Carnegie Foundation? Why not?' Neil replied. 'Carnegie was a Scotsman, and proud of it. This is a Scottish cry for help. If the foundation's taken over his charity work, they'll listen. Even if they say 'no', are we any worse off?'

He turned round to face her. 'But will Aggie write to the doctor?'

'Jonathon? They've been friends all their lives. If one of them got into a scrape, the other jumped in and fought beside them — right or wrong. There was never just one bloody nose. If there was trouble, there was always two. Of course she'll write . . . '

She was suddenly very conscious of standing close to him.

He looked down: her face was an oval blur in the dusk.

He thought he had never known a brighter, or a bonnier woman. Then sensed her face tilt back, her lips rise to meet his own. His arms went around her, without thought. He felt her hands clasp, behind his neck. Their gentle kiss became intense, passionate.

Mary pushed herself away: he made no attempt to draw her back.

'I'm sorry,' she said breathlessly. 'I don't know what . . . '

She sensed him smile. 'I'm not sorry in the least, Mary Cowie,' he said. 'I've been wanting to do that for as long as I can remember.'

'You never said.'

'You never asked.'

'You always seemed such a sober, serious man . . . '

'That's only on the outside.' There was laughter in his voice.

She felt as if she had glimpsed a side to him that she had never known existed. His hands were still holding her arms gently: she liked that. Felt secure, beside his tall shadow. Wanted to burrow in, lay her face against his chest.

Gently, he pushed her away. 'I'd better go. They'll be sailing without me — and the eight of them would starve to death. There's not one can make a sandwich.'

With all her heart, she wanted him to lean down, and kiss her again.

Instead, he raised his finger to his lips, kissed it, and set it gently against her own lips. Where he had touched, began to tingle.

She watched his dark figure walk towards the ships' lights, some of which were already moving down the river. 'Come back safe,' she called after him.

He raised an arm. Then he was just another anonymous dark figure, working with the mooring ropes, casting off from the quay. Mary watched, shivering, as one by one the ships' lights slipped past, down the river, and began to rise to meet the waves of the open sea.

* * *

Chrissie shook her head in resignation. Men!

'You'll be ready for a cup of tea, you two?' she asked.

'Not half!' panted Jonathon.

She pointed an accusing finger at Eric's red face. 'And you're too old to be playing football . . . '

He grinned back at her. 'Not me. I've still a trick or two to show the bairn.'

Jonathon picked up the makeshift ball. 'Where did you learn to do this?' he asked, examining the tightly rolled layers of newspaper, held together by knotted bands of string. It made a ball which was surprisingly light — just ideal for a four-year-old to take a swipe at, and send anywhere. Leaving the two men to chase after his miscues like sheepdogs.

'From my dad. We could never afford a proper ball.'

Small hands reached up to take the ball from Jonathon. It was dropped to meet a mighty kick, glanced off it, and shot sideways into the rose bed.

'Just watch that he doesn't break any windows,' Chrissie sighed.

Rather than wait to see the accident happen, she retreated to her kitchen, shaking her head. As bad as each other, she thought. Men never grew up from being children: scrape away the serious surface, and the unruly boy was usually still inside. She smiled.

What a nice man Jonathon had become. Dropping in, then getting off his jacket and taking over from a purple-faced Eric as chaser-in-chief. Giving wee Tommy the best day he'd known since his mother had gone back to Aberdeen.

What a pity Gus had switched his girls directly down to Eyemouth.

As the tea infused, she moved slowly round her kitchen, reaching up for the biscuit tin, and slicing some homemade cake. She knew that Jonathon would eat his way through anything she set in front of him. Like any man who hadn't a wife to look after him properly.

She glanced through the kitchen window. Without much thought, she could find him a wife. If only — but Aggie was too close: he saw in her a lifelong friend, through thick and thin. Not a woman who was still young and vibrant.

Chrissie sighed. Men were strange. The woman he would choose would appeal to his mind, as well as his senses. Someone like that bonny Cowie quine, who had gone to the war a young girl, and come back a woman, with a mind to match her looks. She would make a perfect doctor's wife — although he'd find her a handful, with all these radical political views. Women's rights indeed! Chrissie sniffed. No sensible woman needed rights, because she should be more than capable of getting her own way — as often as was good for her.

'That's your tea ready!' she called.

They trooped in, Eric mopping his face with a blue handkerchief, Jonathon with a healthy glow of colour on his cheeks. That man didn't take enough time off his work, to play.

'Help yourself to cake,' she encouraged, pouring tea. 'I'll never get the Wee Man calmed down. Having Eric playing with him is bad enough . . . but when there's two of you . . . '

Jonathon took a huge bite of cake. 'He's a nice bairn,' he said, speaking with some difficulty. 'There's not many who would be so happy, without his mum.'

'He has no choice,' Chrissie said bleakly. 'Nor has she.'

'I know.' Jonathon helped himself to another piece of cake. 'I got a letter from Aggie this morning,' he said. 'That's why I'm here. I told you the girls would come up with something that might save us. Well, she has.' He glanced over to Eric. 'She says we should write to the Carnegie Foundation, and ask for their help to buy back the hospital.'

'Carnegie, the steel millionaire?' Eric paused, cup halfway to his mouth.

'What a great idea!' Chrissie exclaimed. 'If anybody can help us, Carnegie's the man. He's built libraries and colleges, all across Scotland.'

'Carnegie's dead,' Jonathon said. 'But his charity work goes on, with Scotland as a major beneficiary.' He handed over the letter. 'I'd never have thought of them. Not in a million years. Aggie did. What a girl! But don't tell her — she's big-headed enough already.'

He looked at Chrissie. 'You can know someone all your life, think you understand every twist and turn of them. Then, one day, they surprise you — it's like seeing them for the very first time. Aggie could have saved the cottage hospital.'

Eric grunted, reading slowly through the letter. 'Aye,' he said. 'But there's a long way to go, before Carnegie's cheque comes through the letterbox. When do the lawyers want us out, to put the house on the market?'

Jonathon winced. 'They've given us until the 3rd of January.'

They stared at each other, calculating. Not quite three months — when it took almost a fortnight for a letter to reach its destination in America. There, to lie on a busy foundation's desk. Then another fortnight for the reply to come back.

'Then we'd better start writing,' Eric said gruffly.

* * *

The *Endeavour* steamed slowly through the harbour entrance, and immediately began to pitch in the turmoil of white waves outside. This October gale had lashed the coast for three full days, keeping all boats in the harbour. Wedged in the deckhouse, Neil tensely watched Andy fighting the steering wheel. The most dangerous time for any boat is when she's close to shore. Here, the backwash from earlier waves sent the incoming waves into steep pyramids, torn apart by the gale, hurling solid water across the deckhouse windows.

Wasn't this what his dad had sent him out to do? Stop Andy from taking reckless actions, which endangered the boat and the lives of his crew? They'd had a tearing argument on land. Watched unhappily by the crew, until they took it with them up into the relative privacy of the deckhouse.

But there was a time and a place for arguing — not when they were clawing their way clear of the harbour walls and the ragged rocks beyond them.

The ship shuddered with every boom of the waves hitting her wooden bows: the hatches were battened down storm-tight, and the crew huddled uneasily in their quarters. With the old engine at full ahead, they were scarcely making headway against the onslaught of the gale and its waves.

The drifter was tossed like a cork as the waves surged under her and past. Yard by yard, she fought clear of the shore, gradually leaving behind the utter madness of confused water outside the harbour. Shaking herself like a wet dog, the old boat settled to the endless battering of waves, driven before the wind.

Andy drew a shuddering breath of relief. 'That was nasty,' he admitted.

Neil shook his head. 'I still think you're crazy. You'll lose your nets and half the crew, if you try to shoot them in seas like this.'

'My choice,' said Andy, peering through the streaming windows. 'There hasn't been a boat out of port in three whole days. We're the only one risking it tonight. This storm can't last forever. If the wind eases off, then the seas will calm down. And if we bring back fish to the market tomorrow, we'll have every merchant bidding for them. We can name our price, turning a fair fishing into a good one in a single night. This old ship has ridden out worse seas than these.'

Neil was silent. Any fish landed would command top price. But was the risk that Andy was taking worth it?

'What's up?' Andy taunted. 'Lost your tongue — or just your courage?'

'So long as that's all we lose,' Neil replied quietly.

The ship buried her bows into the black slope of a huge wave rushing in on them. A couple of feet of white-laced water surged along the rising decks, while the deckhouse windows turned green, then cleared.

'It's a risk worth taking,' Andy muttered.

At times like this, being a skipper was the loneliest job in the world.

* * *

In the cold light of dawn, the wicker baskets holding the samples of the catch of herring gleamed like dull silver. Merchants stood over them, assessing, while the crew of the *Endeavour* got ready to empty the main hold of its fish.

The auctioneer drew his thick coat more tightly about him. It would be a short and a merry round of bidding, he knew. Incomprehensible to any outsider, but he knew every nod, every scratch of an ear, every rub at the side of a nose for the bid it represented. With no sound other than the call of the seabirds and the drone of his voice as the bidding rose, the whole cargo of herrings was sold in a few short minutes. Then the lucky merchants went up to make sure that their quines were happed-up against the weather and ready to start.

Andy watched as the barrows came to wheel his catch away.

Only now would he admit to himself how tired he was. Both from living on the edge for twelve long hours, and from the weight of responsibility he had carried. He came stiffly down the deckhouse steps and walked over to peer down into the now-empty hold. The crew were hosing it down. Job done.

Someone gently squeezed his shoulder. Neil.

'Well,' Andy said tiredly. 'Was I right?'

'So long as you bring back the ship, the skipper's always right,' said Neil.

Andy yawned. 'What that fetched will make even our da crack his face.'

'I doubt it,' Neil replied.

Andy nodded. 'There are some that are born to sing, and others who are born to complain,' he said. 'Which one are you, Neil?'

'For this one time, I'll sing.'

'Because we made it through the storm?'

'That's it,' said Neil.

But he was thinking of the taste and feel of Mary's lips on his.

Andy clapped his back. 'You've had your day,' he said. 'Now all I ask is that you show a bit of trust, and let me have mine. Back then, you were the best skipper on the coast. Like our da was in his day.'

He paused, then said levelly: 'But, by the time I'm finished fishing, I'll be the Findlay that everybody remembers.'

* * *

The whole hospital *felt* better with Aggie and Mary back from Eyemouth, Jonathon thought contentedly: even the handful of patients had perked up. Maybe it was the laughter and energy the girls brought with them. Or the fact that he had given Elspeth the weekend off, to take away a potential source of conflict. A problem he would have to resolve if he persuaded Mary to take the job.

He was whistling as he headed towards the kitchen.

'Typical,' said Aggie. 'You've only got to put the kettle on, and he appears.'

'Just making my routine tour of inspection,' Jonathon said loftily.

'So you won't have time for tea?'

'I didn't say that,' he amended hastily.

He watched her pouring the tea. Still as slim as ever, he noted: and the dark curl was there, exactly where he remembered it, on her neck. As if conscious of his stare, her hand went up to tidy the curl away. She looked up, caught his eyes, and smiled. Then, as quickly as it had come, the smile was gone, her face guarded.

'Any word back from America?' she asked.

'Too soon. The letter has barely reached them. And they're bound to have a system of meetings for dealing with cries for help. We're in a queue and it could be weeks before we get their decision.'

They were both suddenly very aware of the other's presence.

The silence stretched.

It stretched until it broke into Mary's train of thought. She had been wondering where Neil was now, how far down the coast to Yarmouth his old drifter had steamed.

'The Carnegie Foundation?' she said. 'Americans won't hang about. For instance, they've just given all women the vote, like

Canada and New Zealand did in 1919. While we're still stuck with the rule that only women over thirty can vote — when every man, drunk or sober, mad or bad, has been voting for years.'

'I read that news last week,' said Jonathon. He sipped his tea. 'I suppose that hospital of yours was a hot-bed of suffragette ideas.'

'Yes, and no,' Mary replied. 'The surgeons were all sympathizers, part of the drive to break into the medical profession. And most of the young VADs were college girls, who have argued the feminist cause for years. But regular nurses were just nurses, pure and simple. Their main concern was their patients.'

'What about yourself?'

Mary grimaced. 'I'd no interest in politics when I joined up. But the more I learned about the cause, the more it appealed. If a woman can do the same job as a man, why shouldn't she have the same rights?'

'But *can* she do the same job?' Jonathon argued.

'We proved we could,' Mary said. 'Our VAD ambulance drivers collected the wounded and drove them out from the front line, under shell-fire, same as any male orderly. Our surgeons and the nurses worked far closer to the front line than any military hospital. Barely beyond the range of shells.'

'I don't question your courage,' Jonathon came back. 'It's the training which worries me. Elsie Inglis trained her own doctors in that Bruntsfield hospital. Outside the normal medical schools, with their higher standards . . . '

'Higher? Not true!' Mary snapped. 'She turned out women doctors who could pass any examination that the medical schools could set. Because the first thing she taught them was this: to prove they were the equal of any man, they had to demonstrate that they were twice as good. Because they would be under constant hostile observation, and mistakes would never be tolerated.'

'Mmm,' said Jonathon, unconvinced — yet enjoying the argument. 'On the question of the vote, isn't it safer to keep the age for women set at thirty? Making sure that by the time they get the vote, they've had enough experience of life, and its responsibilities, to leave them able to use it sensibly?'

'A good argument,' acknowledged Mary. 'But why not apply *exactly* the same condition to men? Making sure that they have had the same experience of life, and responsibility, to help them use *their* vote wisely and well?'

'Which means not believing in any

politicians' promises,' Aggie interjected.

Jonathon laughed. 'My argument was a two-edged sword,' he admitted. He pushed aside his cup: he was too occupied to drink. 'So your basic argument is that if a job pivots on intelligence and understanding, rather than sheer brute strength, there's no reason why a woman cannot perform as well as any man?'

'Exactly. Now that the war is over, women will challenge professions like the law, banking and business for admission and equal status. Even politics. Some of the girls want to campaign to become Members of Parliament — as the law stands, you can do that at any age, even if you can't vote until you're thirty. It shows the mess of half-thought-out prejudice which men turn into law.'

'MPs like Nancy Astor,' Jonathon mused. 'She took over her husband's seat in . . . where was it . . . Plymouth?'

'She's the first. There will be others. Trust me on that!'

Mary's eyes were flashing: this was a side to her he hadn't seen before, the fierce crusader for women's rights. It both intrigued and shocked him. Like most men of his time, he was conservative by instinct, disliking radical reform. Even when he could see that it was probably needed.

'Equality before the law, for everyone,' he said. 'Great philosophers have argued this, but always from the point of view of men being equal to men. *Liberté, égalité, fraternité* . . . the most wonderful slogan of all. Freedom, equality, and . . . *brotherhood,*' he finished mischievously. He turned to Aggie, smiling. 'What about you, quine? Do you see yourself as the equal of any man?'

'No I don't,' said Aggie. She gathered the dirty dishes. 'I see myself as *better* than any man!'

Jonathon laughed outright. This was a new Aggie. 'I should be holding my head in my hands,' he chuckled. 'What am I going to do with you, how am I going to run this place, with *two* argumentative females for my nurses?'

His smile faded. 'Provided that we still have a hospital to run.'

7

The sea is dangerous — ask any man who makes his living from it. Most of the time, it looks worse than it is. On a very few occasions, when a hollow feeling in your stomach tells you so, it is actually far more dangerous than it looks.

The dark log had been washed overboard from a Finnish vessel in a storm, many weeks before. But the sea is a vast place, leaving it to float in peace like the proverbial needle in a haystack. Only, lying low and solid in the water, it was infinitely more dangerous than any needle.

Dozens of vessels had passed within sight, but none of them had seen it: by now, it was so saturated that it barely broke the surface, lying like a crocodile in an African river. One day, it would wash up onto a beach, and bleach slowly in the sun.

For the moment, it floated. Almost invisible: and utterly lethal.

* * *

Frost made the night air sharp and clear. The small group of friends pulled up their collars and headed back to Yarmouth harbour, laughing.

'It's his walk that makes him funny,' Andy declared.

'No! It's that bendy little walking stick,' said Elsie.

'The baggy trousers?' Aggie offered.

'The man's just a comic genius,' Mary smiled.

Neil said nothing, acutely conscious of the hand that Mary had slipped through his arm. Making him happier than even the Chaplin film had done.

'What do you think, Neil?' she asked.

'I like how he's on the side of the little guy. Against the law . . . against bullies everywhere. We all are, deep inside — that's why we like him. He's smart, and fast on his feet. He always wins.'

He felt her hand squeeze gently. Tucked it tighter still against his ribs.

Andy was in high good humour. It had been his suggestion that they should spend their last few shillings on the picture theatre. 'Watch this,' he said, waving them back as they approached a junction on the road to the docks.

He took a deep breath, and lurched off,

trying to imitate the erratic walk, and the one-legged skidding turn round the corner. On a frozen puddle, his foot slipped out from under him, and he fell with an almighty crash.

The rest of the group howled with laughter.

'That was funnier than Charlie Chaplin,' Aggie gasped. 'Do it again.'

'Are you hurt?' asked Mary, the smile still on her lips.

'Only his dignity,' said Aggie. 'He landed on his wallet.'

Andy scrambled to his feet. To his credit, he was laughing too.

Another figure joined the group. 'That's never Andy Findlay drunk again?' it asked, rocking back slightly on its heels.

'You're a fine one to talk, Gus,' said Aggie, fanning away the smell of whisky.

'It's worrying about you lot that drives me to drink.'

'Then you must have been awful worried,' Mary accused.

'I was,' said Gus. 'I've half of Buckie working for me. Expecting me to buy the fish that makes their wages. And the other half are back at home, expecting me to look after their quines. Saturday night's the only time I can forget my worries.'

Aggie snickered. 'From the state of you, they're forgotten until Tuesday.'

'Not at all,' Gus protested. 'I drink the way my father taught me. Always in moderation — by which he meant no more than one mouthful at a time.'

He fell in alongside them, as they continued down to Fisherman's Quay, where the *Endeavour* was moored, five deep, against other drifters. Every herring boat in Britain was in that harbour by the middle of December.

'Any word from the Carnegie Foundation?' he quietly asked Mary.

She shook her head. 'Not when Jonathon last wrote.'

'They're leaving it late,' Gus said.

'It's getting near the date when we'll have to close the place,' she said. 'Jonathon's decided that he's taking no more in-patients, unless on emergencies.'

Gus grimaced. 'It couldn't have happened at a worse time. Local businesses are like myself — depending on the herring. And landings are still below what they were, before the war. The skippers and their crews are tight for money, so they're buying the bare minimum from chandlers and the like. When fishing sneezes, we all catch cold. Most of the businesses round the harbour are like me — they would break the bank to save the hospital. But it's near broken already.'

They walked glumly down the narrow streets, in darkness between the gas lights. But they knew the way home and there were plenty other groups of fisherfolk, drifting back to their huts or their boats. The real rush home would come later, when the dance halls and the ice rink closed. With surprisingly little trouble, for all the itinerant workers now staying in the town.

It takes money to buy drink, to make trouble: at the end of the final fishing, until payment came, everybody was broke.

'What are you doing tomorrow?' Neil asked quietly. They had fallen behind the others. Her shoulder and arm felt warm and comfortable.

'That depends on where you're going to take me,' Mary smiled up.

Neil touched the few coins in his pocket. Barely enough to jingle.

'We'll think of something,' he said.

And felt her hand snuggle in tighter to his arm.

* * *

The wind was whipping up. In the threadbare light of a December afternoon, the old drifter began to pitch with a more lively action.

Up in the wheelhouse, Neil studied the sky.

He didn't like the look of it, least of all the absence of seabirds anywhere. They had voted with their wings.

'There's a big storm coming in,' he judged.

Andy squinted through the salt-stained windows. 'The settled weather's over,' he grunted. 'About time too. The herrings could see us.'

They had fished all week, barely covering the cost of coal. To make matters worse, today he was facing the indignity that every skipper dreads: a hold completely empty of fish, despite shooting the nets three times overnight, and — in desperation — in the morning too.

'The wind's still north-easterly,' said Neil. 'We could turn and head home in front of it, before it backs round.'

Making a dash for home with the wind behind them made sense. If they left it until one of these big storms came in, the wind would swing right round and by heading west-south-west for Yarmouth, they would be steaming into the full force of the gale, slowing the old boat down to less than walking pace. All sensible fishermen headed for harbour, rather than ride out a storm which filled the North Sea from shore to shore. Leaving no hiding place, no island's lee for shelter.

Andy grunted again. He had never suffered an empty hold before. Sure, it could happen to any skipper. But that didn't stop other skippers and their crews from talking behind their hands. His face burned.

Responsibility lies with the skipper. It's his job to read the sky and the sea, and find herring. If no fish are found then in the eyes of the world, the skipper has failed. Andy shuffled unhappily.

'What are you going to do?' asked Neil. 'The crew are dropping from lack of sleep. We'll never find herring while there's light in the sky. We should get back, before the storm breaks.'

'I hear you,' Andy snapped.

Neil waited, as the silence stretched.

'So?' he prompted.

Andy brought the palm of his hand crashing down onto the wheel.

'Get off my back,' he snarled.

'There's no good steaming further out to sea,' Neil argued. 'It's just leaving more miles to cover when you're fighting back against the storm to get home.'

Andy's whole body radiated anger.

'I'm the skipper of this boat,' he said tightly. 'What we do is my decision.'

A squall came screaming at them, and the drifter buried her bows in an oncoming wave.

Over a foot of white-laced green water swirled down the decks.

'I'm going out to check the hatches,' Neil growled. 'Make sure everything's battened down. Think it through, and do what our da would do. That's what I did, when I wasn't sure, as skipper. But you're right about one thing — the decision is yours alone to make.'

He waited until the squall eased, then opened the deckhouse door and stepped outside. Glancing once again at the sky, he shook his head. This was winter, and the North Sea the most treacherous workplace of them all. When it came at you, its waves were high and steep and often, taxing the boat and its crew to the very limit — and beyond.

Deep in his stomach, he sensed that this was no ordinary storm. He hunched his shoulders, waiting for the best moment to move, then half ran to the bows, catching the rigging, before the next wave broke over him. Shaking himself like a dog, he began to check that the holds were storm-proof.

Back in the deckhouse, Andy bit his lip. Responsibility lay heavy. He was torn between the desire to tough it out and the knowledge that he should be steering towards shelter. He was gambling that he could do again what he had done at Eyemouth. Come back with fish, when the auction market was empty; returning not a loser, but a winner who had nerves of steel.

Against that, he knew that Neil was right. The signs were everywhere. There was a big blow coming up — and they should be making for the safety of a harbour.

If Neil hadn't pushed him, he would probably have turned for home already.

He gripped the wheel, steering into the next wave, which broke in a sheet of solid water over the port quarter. The drifter corkscrewed up, almost vertically, as the wave roared under her. Hesitated at the top, the heavy old propeller screaming as it cleared the water. Then slid, like a sledge, down the back of the wave.

Worth waiting ten more minutes? Andy shook his head wearily: ten minutes would take him no nearer fish in a storm like this. Neil was right — it would only leave them with further to claw back in their flight before the storm. Did it have to be Neil, and did he have to be right? Checking his course on the compass, he calculated that he would need almost a 180-degree turn to head back to safety, and Yarmouth.

Sighing, he braced his legs and spun the wheel.

* * *

'Are they back yet?' Mary asked.

'Who?' Gus's long pointed nose was bright red with cold.

'The Findlay boys. The *Endeavour*.'

Gus frowned. 'The boats have been back for hours. Precious few of them with fish. I never saw Andy, or Neil. If they've drawn blank, they might just have headed straight in to the quay.'

'Right,' said Mary, tightening her shawl around her neck and shoulders. 'I'll nip round and check — thanks, Gus.'

He watched her hurry past the stacks of barrels waiting for shipment. A bonny quine. And sweet on the older Findlay loon: he'd seen them drop back to canoodle at the weekend there.

He sniffed. She could do worse. A solid lad — and one who had found his feet again after coming home from war. Good and bad. If Neil was fully fit again it would leave too much competition for Eric's old boat. Brothers fight — especially when both of them are skippers.

Gus doubted he would see Mary Cowie next year. Not if what he'd heard around the harbour was right. At worst, she'd be the village nurse: at best the wife of the local doctor. A bonny quine, spoiled for choice. And a good worker too. Gus sighed. Next year was five months away, and its problems could wait until then.

Mary hurried down the quay. She blinked, the cold wind bringing tears to her eyes. No sign of the old drifter. She peered across the river. Difficult to be sure, when the drifters were moored together, like a town, floating on the water.

But there was no sign of Neil's boat anywhere. The wind plucked at her shawl. Mary returned slowly to the harbour entrance.

'No luck?' said Gus, still haunting the sheds long after he'd sent his quines back to the relative warmth of their hut.

Mary shook her head. They stood together, staring through the grey gap of the harbour mouth, as the light began to fade. It was almost midwinter, dark by late afternoon. The herring season was almost over. A blast of wind made them stagger.

'God help anybody out there tonight,' Gus said. Then glanced guiltily down at Mary. 'But they'll be safe enough. The Findlays invented the sea, and can cope with anything it throws at them. That's two of our best young skippers, out there.'

Mary nodded silently, pulling the shawl tight again around her shoulders.

'I'll walk you back to the hut,' said Gus. 'It's getting dark.'

* * *

'I can't thank you enough, for coming with me to visit our Jessie,' Chrissie said.

Jonathon scrubbed at his windscreen with a gloved hand. Rain was pouring down, making the glass steam up. 'Happy to help out,' he said. 'I remember your niece well. Her family were my patients for years.'

'That's what she says. And it's her first baby — she's nervous. Her man is away at the fishing. All she needs is a friendly face.'

'Then we can bring her two of those. It's only minutes' work, to check the baby and her blood pressure . . . ' Jonathon leaned forward. 'What a dirty day for anybody to be out in,' he muttered.

'Who?'

'Up ahead. That man, walking.'

Chrissie scrubbed a clear patch on the glass. 'Poor soul,' she said. 'The water's running out of him.'

Jonathon hesitated, then braked to a halt. It was a stranger, a small canvas holdall across his shoulder, greying hair plastered down his face from the rain.

He wound down his window. 'Want a lift?' he called.

The stranger came alongside, bent down, water dripping from his nose. 'That would be just great,' he said. 'This rain of yours is pretty wet.'

The voice was neither Scottish nor American, but had traces of both.

'Climb in,' said Jonathon.

'I'll soak your car,' the man warned.

'It'll soon dry out.'

The small car rocked as the man threw in his bag, then climbed inside.

'Where are you heading?' Chrissie asked, as they moved forward again.

'Portgordon.'

'Us too.' She turned halfway round in her seat, to make talking easier. It was commonplace, men walking their own Roads to Nowhere, restless after the war and this was a decent man, she sensed. Not a tramp.

'Do you live there? Coming home from the war?' she asked.

'I got home from the war over a year ago. I'm not a local, but my grandparents are. I'm over on a visit, and hiking the last few miles to them.'

'American?' Chrissie asked.

'Canadian. My family left here about thirty years ago.'

Chrissie struggled further round. 'What's your grandparents' name?' she asked. 'Maybe I'll know of them.'

White teeth flashed in a weather-beaten

face. 'Campbell. Probably half of the village are Campbells. By the time I find the right ones, it's likely to be midnight.'

'Have you got their address?' asked Jonathon, scrubbing at his windscreen.

'No address. My parents had — but they're both gone. They were the ones who kept in touch with the old folk. I was too busy — like all kids.'

'Did your parents emigrate to Canada from Portgordon?' Jonathon asked.

'They sure did. They left to find work.'

'If they were locals, then you'll have no problem,' Jonathon reassured him. 'Up here, everybody knows everybody else's history. Tell your story to the first people you meet. The chances are they'll take you straight to the door you're looking for. That's how people are up here.'

'My mom always said that too. It's what I'm banking on.'

'You're wet to the skin,' said Chrissie. She'd seen him shiver.

A wry smile. 'I've been wet before. I'll survive.'

Chrissie was a creature of instinct and impulse. 'Look,' she said. 'We're going to my niece's house. Come with us, change into something dry and heat yourself at her fire. Then get a cup of hot tea inside you.'

A pause. 'That's real nice of you,' the man said awkwardly. 'But I couldn't possibly . . . '

'Why not?'

'You don't know me from Adam.'

'What's your name?' demanded Chrissie.

'Angus Campbell. Same as my grandfather — I was named after him.'

'Well, there you are!' she said triumphantly. 'I know you from Adam, now, so you're no longer a stranger. What's more, there can't be many Angus Campbells in Portgordon. My Jessie will know where to send you, once you've dried out. If she doesn't, one of her neighbours will surely know. I'm Chrissie, by the way.'

'Pleased to meet you, Chrissie Bytheway,' he said solemnly, eyes twinkling.

'Get off with you!' she laughed. 'And this man, peering short-sightedly through the windscreen, is Jonathon — our Buckie doctor.'

'It's the condensation,' Jonathon complained. 'Three of us in a small car . . . '

'So you're the doctor?' Campbell said. 'Is somebody ill?'

'Not yet,' said Jonathon cheerfully. 'She's probably healthier than me. Is this where your niece lives, Chrissie?'

'No. Next street down to the sea.' Chrissie wriggled almost three quarters round in her seat, consumed with curiosity. 'What was your mother's maiden name?' she asked. 'Maybe I'll remember her.'

Jonathon caught the Canadian's eye in his rear mirror. 'You'll have to excuse Chrissie, she used to work for the Spanish Inquisition,' he said. 'Until they threw her out for being too nosey . . . '

'That's it!' Chrissie declared. 'I'll tell Jessie no scones, for your cheek.'

Jonathon winked at Campbell. 'On the other hand, she's salt of the earth,' he amended hastily. 'Don't let anybody tell you different.'

Behind him, Angus Campbell's eyes crinkled.

'I wouldn't listen to them,' he said. 'These scones . . . are they anything like the ones my mom used to make?'

* * *

The quines' hut rocked in the squalls raging overhead. It was a wild night and not many were sleeping. It was too noisy and the hut was freezing, bitingly cold, the wind whistling through every crack in the boarding, and every ill-fitting window frame.

Mary lay sleepless, old grey blankets which smelled of dampness wrapped around her.

On her right, Aggie had got up a few minutes before, to find her work jacket and a couple of woollen jerseys: she put the jerseys on, wrapped the blankets round herself, and fell rather than climbed into bed, before reaching out to haul the jacket over her body too.

'This makes Buckie feel like summertime,' she grumbled.

On Mary's other side, Elsie was tossing and turning. With her blankets loosened, there was no chance of building body heat: she shivered, biting her lip to keep her teeth from chattering.

Another blast left the hut timbers groaning, like a ship at sea. And that was the root of Mary's problem. Her mind was on the *Endeavour*. Somewhere out there, miles from the shelter of land, she would be riding out the storm, her old timbers creaking and grunting too.

She moved restlessly. Or had Andy already brought the boat in late, under cover of darkness? Were they moored only a couple of hundred yards away, against the side of another sleeping drifter?

She half sat up, her body ahead of her mind. Should she throw on her shawl, and a pair of boots, go down to see if the boat was back? She was conscious of movement under the shapeless heap that was Aggie, then a long pale arm came out from under the blankets and gripped her hand.

'It's a woman's fate to worry — and the man's job to cope,' Aggie whispered.

'It's such a wild night,' Mary whispered back.

The warm hand squeezed. 'Well, you'd better get used to it. Worrying, I mean. You love that Findlay loon. Don't you?'

Ridiculous. Mary felt her face flush. 'I'm fond of him,' she admitted.

And heard Aggie's snort of laughter.

The bunk beside them stirred, then Elsie was out of it and across. She pulled the blankets from Mary, pushed her over, and climbed in beside her. The girl's body was frozen, and her feet were like ice.

'Are they safe out there?' she whispered.

'Are they ever safe?' Aggie asked bleakly.

'It's just . . . Andy's out there too.'

Mary worked an arm round Elsie's shoulders. 'They'll be fine,' she said, forcing certainty into her voice. A certainty which she didn't feel. 'They're the two best skippers out of Buckie. They'll be here by morning, their holds full.'

The young girl's shivering eased. Within minutes, Mary sensed that she had fallen asleep. So easy when you were young, to trust an older person's judgement, accept it as infallible. She herself felt all too fallible.

'They'll be fine,' whispered Aggie. 'Go to sleep.'

With all her heart, Mary wanted to accept her friend's reassurance. Try as she might, she couldn't. She lay staring sightlessly at the shadowed ceiling.

What was happening, out at sea?

* * *

Jonathon couldn't sleep. As the gale raged round his house, he listened to the squalls. Rain dashed against the window panes. He turned over, trying to find sleep on his other side. Rolled onto his back.

What he needed was to do something, burn off this restlessness. A sense of foreboding possessed him, heavy as a physical weight. He decided to make himself a cup of tea in the kitchen and got up. Reaching for his old dressing gown he wrapped it round himself, yawning, then padded barefoot down the stairs.

Halfway down, he stopped. A brilliant flash of light, then another, streamed through the curtains of the stair window leaving the stairs darker in their wake. He paused on the landing, pulled aside the heavy curtains and looked out.

Far to the south and east, the whole sky lit up, turning the rivulets of rain on the glass into molten silver. Lightning: sheet lightning. He waited for the crash of thunder, but it never came.

The storm must be many miles away, out at sea.

He watched the night sky flaring silently, again and again while the wind screamed and fresh squalls of rain crashed against his window.

The strange silent lightning increased his sense of unease. Lightning you expected in a summer thunderstorm. Not midwinter. He shivered, then closed the curtains and headed down to the kitchen. Even on this side of the house, the room was intermittently lit up by the strange silver-blue flashes of light.

Jonathon closed the internal wooden shutters. They shut out the night, but not the growing sense of unease, foreboding, within him. There seemed something evil, threatening in that distant, silent lightning storm. Superstition, he thought, aware of goose-pimples rising on his body. He was a practising doctor: should be beyond such fears. But, as he filled the kettle, he shook his head.

He wasn't.

The sense of foreboding wouldn't go away:

if anything, it was stronger than before. Something bad was going to happen. He felt it in his bones.

* * *

'Get back to bed,' whispered Aggie. 'Just what good do you expect to do out there? You'll catch your death of cold.'

Mary turned from the window, where the rain streamed down the panes of glass, and the wind shrieked across the gaps in the frame.

'Can't sleep,' she said. 'That lightning, way up north and out to sea.'

Aggie wrestled against the comfort and the heat she had built in the bed, then sighed and began to unwrap clothes and blankets from her body. In her bare feet, she padded over the wooden floor, wrapping the final blanket round herself like a shawl. Then, as an afterthought, when she reached Mary's still figure, she opened the blanket again and wrapped it round the two of them, her warm arms resting on her friend's cold shoulders.

Together they stared through the window, at the almost constant flares of light in the north-eastern sky.

'It's miles away from us,' she said. 'Can't

even hear the thunder. We're safe as houses here . . . '

Mary leaned wearily against her friend, drawing comfort more than heat.

'We're safe,' she said. 'But *they* are out there, the boys. That lightning's miles from us, but they're right in the middle of whatever is causing it.'

Aggie drew her closer as more lightning flared.

'If you're sweet on the loon, you had better get used to feeling this scared and helpless,' she said quietly. 'Like I said, it's the woman's job to worry . . . while she prays to any God who will listen that the boat which holds her man out there, is still riding the waves and afloat . . . '

* * *

Just as Neil had feared, the wind backed west-south-west, rising steadily to storm force ten. It left them plugging dourly into it, deck-house windows streaming from solid water on the outside, and condensation inside. The old boat reeled under the onslaught of steep waves and the screaming blasts of wind.

Three men crowded into her deckhouse. Johnnie had come up to relieve Andy at the wheel, but the skipper refused to go below. So

Neil had brought up a mug of tea — half spilled by the time he reached there — and a salt-sodden sandwich. As Andy wolfed the food and gulped down the tea, he stayed on. Six eyes were better than two, on a night like this when one minute it was pitch black and the next the light so dazzling that they couldn't see.

Neil scrubbed clear a pane of glass. Outside, momentarily, a wall of black water bearing down on them. Then total darkness. There was a dull boom from the bows: the whole ship shuddered, then rose fiercely under the thrust of the wave passing beneath.

At half speed, they were barely making steerage way but to go faster would only increase the battering the ship was taking. Land was still far below a horizon they couldn't see. The storm had them pinned down, like a butterfly on a collector's board. Far to the north, at the centre of the storm, the sky lit up again with vast flashes of sheet lightning. They couldn't hear the thunder for the bedlam outside.

Andy handed back the empty plate and mug.

'I'll take the wheel,' he said wearily.

Johnnie hesitated. 'You've had the watch for hours already, Skipper,' he said.

'I'm fine,' Andy snapped.

‘Johnnie’s right,’ Neil said. ‘We’re safe enough out here. Stuck, until the storm blows itself out. We’re marking time. You won’t get a better chance to rest.’

‘The skipper stays on deck . . . ’ Andy argued.

‘An exhausted skipper is no use to man nor beast,’ Neil said. ‘Get your head down for an hour. We can’t do anything different from what we’re doing. Not even by dawn. I’ll keep watch up here, with Johnnie.’

Andy frowned. The thought of crawling into a damp bunk and closing his eyes for a few minutes was sorely tempting. Neil was right: they could do no more than keep their bows to the onslaught of the waves. To turn and flee in front of the storm was to leave even more miles between them and Yarmouth, when he was already doing sums in his head about the coal in the engine room bunker.

‘Go on, Skip,’ Johnnie urged. ‘We’ll be fine.’

Another huge wave came roaring in from the dark, burying the *Endeavour*’s bows, then sending her soaring skywards. Black seawater swept along the deck and engulfed the foot of the deckhouse.

‘Just watch yourself going back,’ warned Neil.

Not idle advice. It had been a mouth-drying dash from the crew’s quarters round to the deckhouse stairs when he brought

Andy's sandwich and tea. There were no safety harnesses — or even safety ropes — on these old fishing boats.

Andy yawned, peering out into darkness beyond the feeble cocoon of light on deck. 'Right. You take the watch, Johnnie. No need for you to hang around up here, Neil. Get your head down too. We'll need our wits about us in the morning.'

He waited until another wave surged past then slipped through the deckhouse door. Halfway down the short stair, as the *Endeavour* slid down the rear slope of the wave, he paused. Looking up, uncertainly, as if he sensed . . .

The *Endeavour* hit something solid in the water. She stopped dead in her tracks, as the next wave roared in and underneath.

Andy, his attention split between the boat and himself, pitched headfirst over the rail into the winch housing. Then was picked up by the surging water and slammed against the foot of the deckhouse stairs, and swept aft to the stern rail.

* * *

Mary sat bolt upright in the bed. At her side, Elsie grumbled and tugged back the bed-clothes. In the darkness, Mary's head was spinning, her heartbeat thundering in her chest. Half awake, she felt nauseous and frightened to death.

Wrapping her arms around herself, she listened to the wind scream over them, while the old shed grated and creaked. Gradually, her heartbeat slowed and she struggled to take control over her mind again. She shivered, as another squall rocked the hut. If it was like this on land, what would it be like out there?

It had felt like a dream, only it wasn't. The image burned in her mind was too clear for any dream. Something terrible had just happened, out at sea . . .

Leaving Neil and the crew now fighting for their lives.

* * *

Neil was out of the deckhouse before he'd fully registered what had happened. He vaulted the rail and landed in the slack of the wave's surge. Saw Andy being swept overboard, and launched himself after his brother's tumbling body. They slammed into the stern rail together. Wind and sea clawing at them.

Neil grabbed two fistfuls of Andy's jacket. Jamming his feet against a stanchion, he surged clear with all his strength, fighting to reach the comparative lea of the deckhouse and the crew's quarters.

No good. Another swirling wall of seawater drove him back. He flung himself sideways, and crashed against the lifeboat mounting. With one arm, he grabbed it desperately, fighting to get his feet beneath him.

While holding grimly on to Andy with his other hand.

The trailing body was nearly sucked away. Neil's shoulders cracked, but he held on. Then Andy became an inert burden, too heavy to let him move quickly — leaving them both exposed to the surges of water along the decks.

Bracing himself against the mast, he dragged Andy closer. Waited for the wave to pass, then launched himself desperately across the heaving deck towards the crew's quarters. Andy's body was a deadweight, slowing them as the next wall of water came coursing along the deck.

The door opened, and two crewmen rushed out. This time it was four bodies which tumbled back towards the stern, and the sea beyond. But three desperate men are stronger than one. Their slide stopped as they crashed into and half under the lifeboat, leaving them bruised and breathless.

Dragging Andy towards the open door, they tumbled inside and down the short stairs. The floor was swimming.

'Close that door,' Neil gasped. 'We'll be swamped.'

The rest of the crew were scrambling out of their bunks, while the lantern swung wildly under the low roof. Neil turned Andy over. Blood ran with salt seawater down the white, young face. His brother was unconscious — or dead.

He felt for the artery in the throat: Andy's heart was beating.

What injuries? And quickly, because whatever had hit the *Endeavour* had left her mortally wounded. Even with less than half his attention, he felt her rising ever more sluggishly to the thrust of the waves.

Gently, he felt round Andy's head. His hands came away red.

Neil slowly turned the head round. A huge tear, from the crown down behind the right ear. He hesitated, then gently felt the skull beneath. Fearing — even expecting — movement of the bone after a blow like that. The skull was intact.

He released breath that he seemed to have been holding for days.

'He's knocked out. Get him onto a bunk,' he growled.

'What happened to us?' one of the crewmen asked, as they lifted Andy onto the nearest bunk.

'We hit timber or something in the water,' Neil said. 'One of you, get up there to the deckhouse and ask Johnnie how the ship is coping.'

'Right, Skip.'

Neil didn't notice.

'Donald. You and Davie bandage his head. Try to draw the edges of the tear together. I'm going down to the engine room and through to the hull, to find out what the damage is.'

'Aye, aye, Skip.'

Neil stared. No time to argue.

He patted Andy's cheek, then hurtled down the stairs into the engine room. No sign of the engineer.

'Padraig!' he yelled.

'Up forr'ard!' the voice was faint.

Neil ducked into the dark. He knew every nook and cranny of this ship: as a boy, he had explored, every space. Beyond the main hold, he saw the faint glow of an oil lantern. Padraig. On his hands and knees, he eased into the cramped V of the hull, through slopping water almost two feet deep.

The big Irishman pointed. In the light of the lantern, seawater was gushing in through bow planks which had been sprung, maybe even shattered.

'We're shipping water,' he said calmly.

'Are the timbers holed?'

'There's three planks sprung. About four feet of damage. Whatever we hit, it was a glancing blow.'

'Repairable?' Neil gingerly felt the extent of the gaps.

'At sea? In these conditions?'

Around them, water rose steadily.

'When this reaches the engine room, it'll dowse the boiler,' Padraig warned.

Leaving them without power. Drifting completely at the mercy of the storm.

Worse still, going down.

Padraig looked at him wryly. 'I thought I would live forever, after getting through the Somme. No more bullets with my name on them.' He grimaced, his wet face shining grotesquely above the lantern. 'Nobody ever said about my name on a floating log.'

'The men,' said Neil. 'We'd better get back to them.'

The level of water inside the bows was rising quickly, and the engine room was already flooding, greasy water and steam swirling round. Dripping oil and water, they climbed into the crew's quarters, to meet the stares of the waiting crew.

'Planks sprung, on the starboard bow,' Neil said grimly. 'Shipping water.'

A silence. Then Davie spoke.

'The boys want to take to the lifeboat. Launch her over the stern.'

Neil shook his head. 'In these seas, we wouldn't last ten minutes.'

'Then what do we do?'

He heard the panic, controlled by iron courage, in Davie's voice.

So much like the voices of the men he had led in the trenches. Men who knew they were facing certain death. But were determined to meet it like men. To die without shame.

'We stay with the ship,' he growled. 'Keep her afloat . . . patch her up.'

'How?'

Their eyes watched him, whites reflected in the swinging lantern's light.

It was his responsibility. A familiar burden, settling on his shoulders. He sensed, rather than heard, the engine stop.

'The boiler's gone out,' said Padraig. 'We need a miracle now . . . '

8

With Andy unconscious, Neil found himself moving seamlessly from cook, back to skipper of the boat. The responsibility and decisions were his alone.

First things first: the boat had to be brought under control. That meant getting steerage way — with his engine dead. And the only way to do this was to hoist the small stern sail, which all drifters used to let them hold station while waiting for their nets to fill.

'Davie. Hoist the stern sail,' he snapped. 'Not full up or the wind will blow it to shreds. Just enough to give us steerage. Take Dougie — and keep an eye on these waves, both of you.'

'Aye, aye, Skip.'

'Donald. Get back to Johnnie. Tell him to come about, between the waves, as soon as we have steerage way. Then set our stern to them . . . '

A risk. Taking big seas over the stern could founder them: but doing nothing condemned them to sinking like a stone.

'Padraig. We're going into that hull again.

Bring the blankets from the bunks — and the broadest-bladed chisel you can find.'

'Right, Skip.'

'The rest of you, get pails and buckets. Make a human chain from the engine room to the deck. Bail for your lives — but have a man on that door to close it fast, if he sees us being swamped by a wave.'

In the lantern light, their faces were yellow and grim. Set in stone, because they were fighting for their lives in this old boat — and there wasn't a man who didn't know it.

'Get on with it, boys. Good luck,' he snapped.

'What about Andy?' Dugald asked.

'Leave him to come back to his senses. We need all hands.'

Dragging, an armful of blankets, Neil fought back through the spaces into the bows. Water everywhere, waist deep rising to chest deep, slopping and surging as the *Endeavour* wallowed sluggishly in the path of the waves.

Jammed into the constricted space of the bows, with Padraig holding a lantern for light, Neil growled: 'An old deep-sea sailorman told me this. If they were holed at sea they tried to work a sail under the boat's hull. The water pressure held it tight, and slowed down the inflow. Then they packed the hole from inside with sails or blankets, and nailed it down. It still leaked, but they could usually cope by bailing out.'

He took a deep breath. 'We're not holed. So, maybe if we can stuff blankets between each plank that's sprung, and tamp them in with a chisel . . . '

'Like caulking the planks again?'

Neil nodded. 'It might just work.'

Padraig silently handed over the first blanket. Neil folded it once, then twice. By touch, he found the end of two planks where the flow of water rushed past his fingers. Traced the gap back until he could almost fit his fingers between the planks. Groping under water, he started feeding the blanket into the gap. Then punched it tight with the broad-bladed chisel that Padraig had brought.

The first planks were easy: then, as he worked deeper, he had to hold his breath and duck his head under to reach then repair the damage.

The water was freezing cold. Dulling his mind, not his will. No feeling in his hands, but he barely noticed. Pain from splinters disappeared. His whole existence revolved round feeling, sensing, jamming the coarse fabric into gaps, then ramming it home hard. Then surfacing, spent and gasping, his breath pluming out in the lantern light, while water coursed off his face.

Their last blanket filled the last gap. Just.

Neil was utterly spent. 'Padraig,' he gasped. 'You come here and feel if there's any water rushing in. If there isn't, tamp everything in as hard as you can manage with that chisel.'

They struggled past each other. Neil fought not to drop the lantern, his breath still whooping, and his body in shuddering spasm.

Then Padraig looked up, filthy-faced but exultant. 'We're sound, Neil,' he panted. 'If I ever meet your sailorman, I'm going to buy him as much as the old bugger can drink.'

'Then you'll have to dig him up first,' Neil replied, teeth chattering. He lowered the lantern. 'Right. If the lads have got the stern sail working, our next job is just to bail and bail, until the water level falls. Could take all night, even tomorrow. Then light the boiler fire again — that won't be easy. Once we have the engine working, we can turn for home. But at dead slow — otherwise that caulking will never hold.'

He scrubbed his eyes. 'Is there anything I've forgotten?'

Padraig grinned, demonic in the lantern's light.

'Yes,' he said. 'We can pray.'

* * *

'Don't try to do too much,' Jonathon said. 'Especially over the first week . . . ' He stood in the doorway of the now-empty cottage hospital, watching the husband and wife walk slowly downhill to the town. Last patient gone, quicker than he would have preferred. In effect, thrown out of the cottage hospital whose sole mission it was to look after them. But what choice was there?

The letter from America was burning his hand: just delivered, as he escorted the woman and her husband through the door. He was desperate to open it, but waited to wave. Neither of the couple looked back.

Closing the door, he threw the rest of the mail onto the desk inside the hallway. Now that the letter was in his hands, he was afraid to open it.

Sticking a finger inside the envelope flap he tried to ease it away. No good: this was an expensive envelope with sound adhesive. He fumbled for his letter-knife in the desk drawer, and cut through the flap.

The empty envelope fluttered to the floor.

Jonathon's eyes raced down the page: 'Oh, God,' he said.

This was what that premonition, two nights before, had heralded.

Disaster, but the others would have to know. Grabbing a coat, he rushed through the door, leaving the envelope discarded on the carpet. The front door banged shut: no time to lock it. He threw his coat into the rear of the car, and went round to begin the prolonged business of starting it.

When the engine fired, he climbed in, closed the door and nudged the car into gear. Then accelerated down the hill, passing the couple who were walking slowly home. They looked at each other in surprise. Not like the doctor to go past them: he must have something all-absorbing on his mind.

Jonathon brought the little car to an untidy skidding halt outside Eric's door and gathered up the letter. Knocking, he walked straight inside, as if he was on a house call, re-reading the letter.

The contents hadn't changed. They never would. Not now.

'What's up?' asked Eric, startled out of forty winks. 'Oh . . . ' He had seen Jonathon's face.

'Read this,' Jonathon held out the letter.

'I can't,' Eric replied. 'My specs are in the kitchen. Read it to me.'

Jonathon turned the letter round, and studied it. 'Very friendly,' he said. 'Lots of stuff about Andrew Carnegie's pride in his Scottish ancestry, how interested he would have been. Then, the important bit:

'We have considered your request for help at considerable length, as we know our founder would have done. There are two major issues which influence our response. Firstly, the Foundation's remit is to promote the advancement and diffusion of knowledge and understanding: not provide funds for buildings. Secondly, while we are happy to consider an unusual project, we feel bound by our founder's own basic principles. Andrew Carnegie started life as a bobbin boy in a cotton factory. He reached where he did by dedicated part-time study. His objective was to help others to travel that same path, to freedom. Thus his charity gifts were tied to funding colleges, and libraries, places where an ordinary working lad could study to improve himself. A cottage hospital, worthy though it is, scarcely falls into any of these categories. Regretfully, we must turn your request for funding assistance down.

However, we do not wish to abandon both your cause and your community — both of which deserve better. We have sent your letter on to a friend of his — another Scot who came to the New World with only the clothes he wore, but has made his fortune in timber. We have asked if he can help you. At some future date, he may be in touch' . . . '

Jonathon looked up blindly. 'It has taken two months for Andrew Carnegie's foundation to reply. If his friend ever decides to help — and why should he? — it's going to come too late. The building's up for sale in ten days' time.'

'Come through to the kitchen, and I'll make us a cup of tea,' Eric said heavily. 'Let me see that letter . . . where are my specs?' The old fisherman read the text, slowly and deliberately. 'They sound nice people,' he judged.

'But not nice enough,' said Jonathon. 'What do we do now?'

Eric thoughtfully reached for his pipe and tobacco tin. Took out a flake of tobacco, and began to rub it between the heels of his hands. Unusually, some of the crumbled tobacco fell to the floor.

Jonathon saw that the old man's hands were shaking.

Eric stuffed the tobacco slowly into his pipe. Began his search for the matchbox, which lay in full view beside the tobacco tin. Wordlessly, Jonathon reached over and handed him the matches. Eric struck one and held it over the bowl of his pipe. Smoke wreathed his face.

Then he took the pipe away, and flapped out the match.

'You make the tea,' he said gruffly. 'I'll fetch Chrissie — she should know. The quines are back tomorrow. Maybe they can think of something.' He looked up, blindly. 'What's going to happen to the town?'

Jonathon sighed. 'That was our last chance . . . and it's gone, taking the cottage hospital with it.'

* * *

The storm blew itself out — bringing down the final curtain on the herring season. Any drifters leaving the harbour now were generally heading home for Christmas if they were English boats, or New Year if they were Scottish.

The communal huts were emptying, faster than they'd filled. Each merchant was busy making payments for the fishing, then arranging for his gutting teams to travel home.

Aggie was in a ferment about buying something before they left, to take home to her Wee Man. Quines sang and stuffed their filthy belongings into kitbags and ancient leather cases — to be washed, once they were home again. Only Elsie sat, head bowed and miserable, on the edge of her bed.

Gus paused in the doorway. 'Mary Cowie's team?' he asked. One of the quines pointed inside and he entered, uncomfortably edging round the young women and heading for Aggie.

'I've got your rail tickets,' he addressed her busy back.

She straightened quickly. 'Any news?'

Gus shook his head, frowned, and nodded over to Elsie.

'Where's Mary?' he asked.

Aggie sighed. 'Down at the pier head. Where else?'

Gus glanced at the neat, but empty bed. 'Is she packed?' he asked.

Aggie shook her head silently.

'She's not going home,' said Elsie. 'And neither am I. Not until . . . '

Then her head bowed, and her shoulders started shaking.

Aggie walked over, put her arm silently round the girl's shoulders.

'We're all going home together,' Gus said firmly. 'Your families would have me thrown out of Buckie if I left you here.'

'You'd better see Mary,' Aggie said. 'I'll stay with Elsie, for a bit. Just don't take forever . . . '

'We haven't got forever,' Gus snapped. 'Our train leaves at 4 p.m.'

'I'm staying, with Mary,' Elsie's muffled voice declared.

Gus puffed out his cheeks. No wonder he was single: looking after everybody else's quines soon turned a man into a monk. He strode towards the harbour. Mary would be keeping her lonely vigil there, long after the rest of the world knew that it was too late for the *Endeavour* to come back. Not after she was three days overdue — an old vessel, out in the worst storm to hit the coast in years.

He saw Mary's beshawled figure staring out to sea, as she had done throughout the daylight hours. It was a damned shame. His heart ached for the girl, and he liked the Findlay boys. But there came a time when hope and prayer had to stop, and life must move on without them.

Gus walked up to her, his eyes on the grey sea stretching out to a cold horizon, straight as a pencil line drawn by a ruler.

'They won't be coming back,' he said at last. 'Not now.'

She didn't answer.

'There's nothing to be served by staying here. Locals know this stretch of sea. If she'd survived, they say the *Endeavour* would be back, by now.'

Still she didn't reply.

'The Fraserburgh and Buckie lads promised me that they'd spread out and comb the fishing grounds, on their way north. If they found anything, somebody would have come back to tell us.'

Mary blinked.

'You can't just hold a one-person wake,' Gus argued. 'I've got the tickets. We're all going home at four this afternoon. Then the night train north. You'll be in Buckie with the milk, tomorrow morning.'

'I'm staying here,' Mary said quietly.

'What good will it do?' he demanded. 'It won't bring them back.'

'I'm staying on. You take the girls.'

'If you stay here, then Elsie will stay here too. That crush on Andy . . . she's just a girl, a school lass barely. You cannae give her the excuse to stay behind. What will her family say?'

'She's a woman now. She can make up her own mind. I'm staying.'

'Aggie's got your tickets. She's desperate to get back, to her little boy.'

Mary blinked again.

'Come on,' Gus pleaded. 'This isn't Buckie. The Findlay's boat hasn't disappeared in the Moray Firth. We can't keep a vigil for her, like we would, up there. If they're still afloat, they'll be found. If they aren't found, if they don't come limping back . . . then they're gone. It makes no difference whether you stand here, waiting, or come back home.'

'It makes a difference to me,' said Mary. 'And maybe, just maybe, it will make a difference to them too.'

Gus threw up his hands. 'You can't keep them alive by willpower alone, Mary! This is the sea you're dealing with. We live by her and, if she gets tired of us, we die by her. Men disappear, become only memories — whatever we'd rather have.'

'I'm staying,' said Mary.

'And I'm responsible for four teams of quines, and getting them back to Buckie tomorrow morning. I can't keep them here and change the tickets, waiting until you finally give up.'

'I'm staying on,' said Mary.

The iron in her voice reflecting the iron in her will.

* * *

She edged over the grey horizon, so tiny against the vastness of the sea that even watching for her, Mary didn't think it was a boat. She screened her eyes, her heart hammering. Then the tears began to flow, making it impossible to see clearly, when clear vision was needed to be certain.

Mary watched, and waited. Terrified that the next time she wiped the tears from her eyes, the tiny dot would have disappeared.

It stayed stubbornly solid, travelling so slowly that time ground to a halt: a fishing boat, limping towards Yarmouth harbour, when everyone else was heading home. It could have been one of these, run into trouble. But Mary knew with total certainty that it was the *Endeavour*, bringing Neil safely back.

She flew from the pier head to their hut, crashing through the doorway, to find the place almost deserted. Only the few Buckie teams were left, sitting on the stripped beds, kitbags and cases at their feet.

'They're back!' she shouted. 'Our boys. They're coming home . . . '

Elsie covered her face. Aggie threw her arms round Mary, and hugged her tightly. Then Elsie was off like a fawn, swooping down to tell Gus, leaving him far behind her flying feet as she raced down to the harbour mouth.

The women poured out into the cold, shouting, skirling. It was a Buckie boat, with Buckie loons, and there would be Buckie women waiting to cheer them home. They overtook Gus, tears streaming down his face.

Aggie scooped him up into the crowd of women.

'Look at you!' she scolded. 'Greeting, worse than any bairn.'

'You're greeting too,' he snuffled, long red nose shining.

'I'm a woman,' she said. 'I'm entitled to greet.'

'And I've been with women far too long,' sighed Gus.

In a tight-knit band, they marched down to the harbour. With most of the fishing boats gone from the quays, the place seemed empty. But local fishermen, colliers, and fish merchants shouted to ask what the news was, then dropped their work and followed too. The sea was a common foe, and any boat saved from her an occasion for delight. Within minutes, the harbour mouth was lined with people. The quines pushed through to reach Elsie at the uttermost point of the harbour, where she was skipping and dancing, like a madwoman — and nobody cared.

As she approached, everyone saw how low in the water the *Endeavour* was, travelling at a speed which barely made a ripple round her bows. When she limped into the harbour entrance, they saw the chain of weary men on deck, bailing endlessly, returning seawater to the sea.

Somewhere inside the harbour, a vessel started blasting her foghorn — its celebration taken up by others. While the waiting crowds began to wave, and cheer. The sea seldom releases her victims — but this one had made it home.

The deckhands stopped bailing, surprised by the welcome they were being given. A couple of them waved back, self-consciously: then the chain of buckets coming up took over again. The temporary caulking with blankets had slowed the leak but the longer they had edged through the sea, the less effective the repair had become. So the crew were working just to keep the water level where it was.

Whoever was steering had the presence of mind to head straight for the ramp of the dry dock, with the tide on the ebb. The cheering crowd following the *Endeavour* in. Men fought to catch the warps thrown up to them, then watched as the dry dock team manoeuvred a cradle under the hull. She would be left to drain, before being winched into the dock to be repaired.

Mary pushed through the watching crowd. Neil was standing outside the deckhouse, his faced lined with dirt and exhaustion. The sunken eyes lit up when he saw her.

'Mary Cowie!' he called up. 'Come aboard. We need a doctor.'

Fishermen never allowed a woman to step on board their vessel: it brought bad luck. So whatever the problem, it was serious. The cheers died away, and Mary was helped down onto the steel ladder below the lip of the quay, its rusty rungs rough on her hands.

She felt herself steadied, and turned to find Neil towering over her: 'Thank God you're safe,' she said quietly. 'Who's hurt?'

Neil scrubbed his face. 'It's Andy,' he said.

There was a wail from above.

'He's taken a bad blow to the head. He's sick and confused. And I think a couple of ribs have gone. He's lost a lot of blood . . . but at least he isn't coughing it.'

'Let me see him,' Mary said.

They guided her to the crew's quarters, where Andy was lying, ashen faced and childlike, in a bunk. Mary took a deep breath, and kneeled to examine the torn skin, now clotted with congealed blood.

'He needs a doctor, but I can clean the wound,' she said. Gently, she palpated the skull. 'We're best having X-ray plates taken, to make sure the skull hasn't fractured raggedly inside. But it feels sound. He's a lucky boy.'

She looked up. 'Gus will know who to ask for a charabanc to run Andy to the infirmary. Ribs too, you said . . . ' As she spoke, her hands moved gently down. Andy groaned.

The quayside was so quiet that many of the watchers heard. Gus was already running to the harbour master's office and its telephone. Elsie was struggling to get down, but the Buckie women were gently holding her back.

Mary straightened. 'What happened?' she asked.

Neil wiped his face with a filthy hand. 'We hit something big and heavy, floating in the water. Luckily, we weren't holed — or we wouldn't be here now. And if that storm had lasted a few hours more, our repair would never have held. We were blown miles off course.'

'But you brought them home,' she said. Aching to hug him tight.

'I brought them home,' he said wearily.

Then his back straightened, as if a giant burden had gone. 'This time, I really brought them home,' he said, wonder in his voice.

In his mind's eye, a series of flashes from shell explosions. Mud and torn bodies everywhere. Barbed wire. Broken, skeletal trees. Raw ruins of farmhouses. Muddy faces of the youngsters with him, shining in the flares of battle. The faces of boys who would soon die, and horribly, whatever he did to try and save them.

The shakes came out of nowhere, like they always did.

'We'll look after him,' Padraig said gruffly. 'These shakes don't bother us. He's our skipper, and he brought us home.'

* * *

On the station platform, there was an awkwardness between them which Mary neither understood, nor wanted. But he was back and, for the moment, she was content.

'You should be up at the hospital, with Andy,' she scolded.

Neil tried to stifle a yawn. Couldn't. 'I'll go, as soon as your train has left,' he promised. Then fought another yawn.

'When did you last sleep?' she asked.

'Not since we struck that bit of timber.'

That was two, even three days ago: no wonder he looked exhausted.

She wanted to be in his arms, not chatting quietly at his side. The other Buckie women had made room for them and were further down the platform — watching from the tails of their eyes, no doubt. She didn't care.

She had thought that his first act would be to pick her up and smother her with kisses.

Mary was aching to abandon herself within his arms. Yet they were standing here as friends — or even strangers.

'What's up, Neil?' she asked him quietly.

That familiar level look: this wasn't a man who shirked a question.

'When you think you're going to die, your survival instinct takes over,' he said slowly. 'You fight to save yourself and the people round you. But part of your mind is standing back, thinking. I thought of you, of where the two of us were heading. Knowing that, if I let things run, I was condemning you to a lifetime of standing on cold quays, and waiting for a late boat to come in. Or lying sleepless with worry, every night.'

'That's what fisherwomen do,' she replied.

'You're capable of so much better than that,' Neil said quietly. So quietly, she had to strain to hear above the other noises in the station.

'My choice,' she said.

'Then you'd be wrong. You'd be betraying yourself.'

'What do you mean?'

His eyes bored into her. 'You have it in you to do something great — something you can be proud of, for the rest of your life. You could study medicine. Become one of these pioneer women doctors you were talking about. Fight for women's place in the medical profession. Open the door for other women, everywhere. You have the brains — and the courage for it. You would be wasting your life if you did anything less.'

A cold hand gripped Mary's heart. She shivered.

He gently held her arms. 'I'm the very thing you should be avoiding like the plague. An ordinary fisherman. Because if you come to me, you will know nothing other than poverty. The only marks you would leave in this sad world would be your headstone, and your family. What a waste of the gifts you have been given, Mary Cowie.'

'My choice,' she repeated thickly. 'What if that's all I want to be?'

The tired eyes crinkled. 'It's my choice too. And I choose to send you back to your cottage hospital. And with every fibre of my being, I urge you to do more than be a nurse there. Use it as your stepping stone. As a marker along your path to becoming a doctor.'

'Mary. It's our train,' said Aggie, touching her arm.

She hadn't noticed it come in.

'Neil Findlay . . . ' Her voice was pinched and hurting. 'When you bring that ship of yours back to Buckie, I'll be waiting for you.'

He pushed her gently away. 'Don't, Mary. Because I won't be looking for you on the quay. I refuse to be the millstone that grinds you down.'

Long after the train moved off, and its clouds of smoke and steam had dispersed, he stood there. Alone, on the platform. Looking down the shining rails that were the start of the quines' long trip home. His face was tired, but set: if his heart was hurting, there was not a man — or woman — would ever read that in his face. Seagulls wheeled and called above the station.

Slowly, he turned away. Then began the long walk to the hospital.

* * *

Jonathon rubbed condensation from the windscreen of his car. Another emergency night call, to a house he'd never visited before in Portgordon. In the dark, he'd followed the woman's instructions: this was roughly where her house should be. Had she left the shutters open, as he'd asked, letting the light from her oil lamp shine like a beacon through the dark?

There: down to the far right of a lane. He left the car and walked briskly towards the house, closing the lapels of his coat against the wind with his free hand. Then knocked on the house door and went in.

Old worried faces. Threadbare dressing gowns thrown hastily over nightclothes. An air of panic, barely under control.

'Where's the patient?' he asked briskly.

'Up in the guest room, Doctor.'

Probably the children's bedroom, empty after the flock had flown, under a steep roof with a tiny attic window. It was.

Jonathon blinked. 'We meet again,' he said.

Angus Campbell grimaced. 'I can think of better circumstances.'

'What's the problem?'

Campbell groaned, sinking back onto the bed. 'Gut ache, like I have never known before,' he said tightly.

'May I?' Jonathon lifted the blankets away, then opened the man's pyjama jacket. 'Where is the pain?' he asked.

Campbell's hand gingerly traced the area. 'Started down here . . . then switched to the centre of my stomach. Came in waves. I thought it was something I'd eaten. Cramps.'

'When was this?'

'Started a day or so ago. My granddad gave me bicarbonate of soda, but it didn't help. The pain's got worse. It's unbearable now . . . here . . . '

Campbell touched the lower right side of his abdomen.

Many ailments might trigger and follow these symptoms. Appendix problems, obviously: but there were others.

'Let's take your temperature,' Jonathon reached into his old Gladstone bag and brought out the thermometer case. He gently flapped the instrument, to neutralize the reading. 'Slip this under your tongue.'

He turned to the old man in the doorway: 'When did he last eat?'

'He's had nothing since his dinner, yesterday.'

Dinner — that meant lunch. Midday.

'Has he been sick?'

Shake of the head.

'Starting to feel queasy now,' Campbell mumbled.

Jonathon checked the temperature reading: very high. 'Do you feel fevered?' he asked.

'I'm swinging between sweating, and shivering.'

Campbell's body bucked, as a wave of pain hit. Sweat ran down his face — ivory yellow, unlike the weatherbeaten skin Jonathon remembered.

Not good. He didn't like the way the symptoms were adding up. 'Let's check your abdomen,' he said, rubbing his hands briskly together, then down the sides of his trousers, to generate some heat. 'The doctor's curse,' he smiled. 'Cold hands.'

'I'm past caring,' Campbell said.

Jonathon gently palpated the abdomen. As he suspected, reasonably normal lower left quadrant: and upper left. But muscles rigid and tensed anywhere near the lower right. Almost certainly appendicitis — even if the man was older than the normal range.

Surgery was needed: with the cottage hospital as good as closed and the nurse away. Jonathon straightened. Highland doctors had often done the job on kitchen tables. He could manage better than that.

He sniffed Campbell's breath: it was rank. Another symptom. Gently, he palpated the abdomen again. It might be imagination, or Campbell tensing in anticipation of pain, but the rigidity had increased. Muscles contracting in the abdomen wall? If so, not good at all.

More than a day of steadily increasing pain? This man could be very sick indeed: peritonitis — the ruptured appendix infecting the membrane of the abdomen, and a killer if it wasn't treated quickly.

He checked his pocket watch. Coming up to 5.30 a.m.

Campbell groaned again.

Jonathon sat on the bed. 'You need to be hospitalized,' he said bluntly. 'I'm diagnosing appendicitis. The hospital best equipped to deal with this is over an hour away in Elgin. We've a local cottage hospital in Buckie, where I can do the surgery. If we act quickly, it's a routine procedure. But I'm in the middle of closing the cottage hospital down — we have to be out of the building in a few days' time. So I will have to arrange a transfer for you, to either Banff or Elgin. But by then, the crisis will be over.'

'Can't it wait until I get home?' Campbell asked.

'Quite impossible.'

'That serious?'

'Not yet. But if we don't act fast, it might be. I'm not prepared to take that chance.'

Campbell grimaced. 'Hospitals spook me. I spent weeks in one with a smashed leg once. But I don't have any choice, do I?'

Jonathon silently shook his head.

Campbell sighed. 'Your call, Doc. I'm in your hands.'

Jonathon stood up, his mind already racing ahead.

'I'll fetch my car,' he said.

* * *

If the problem was appendicitis, then he could do the job himself, Jonathon thought. No need to bring back the nurse until later. He could anaesthetize, make the incision, fumble around for the appendix, remove it, seal the intestinal opening, stitch everything up. But peritonitis . . . even if he brought her back, would the nurse be capable of assisting?

One step at a time. Hospitalize the man, prepare both him and the theatre. Then take it from there.

As Jonathon headed through the town, he braked suddenly. A group of fisherwomen in shawls were trudging from the station, cases or kitbags in their hands.

'Mary!' he shouted over. 'Can you come up to the hospital and assist? Right now? I need a theatre sister — and there's nobody I'd rather choose.'

She came over, looking as if she hadn't slept in days.

'What procedure?' she asked, her mind sharp as ever.

'Appendectomy. Possible peritoneum infection.'

She nodded. 'I can help. A lot of the shell wounds meant surgery and cleansing in the abdominal area.' She glanced at Campbell, reading the same symptoms that had brought worry-lines to Jonathon's face. 'I'll get into the back,' she said. 'The girls can look after my kitbag.'

'Can I help too?' Aggie; scared, tired, and pale. But willing.

'Squeeze in with Mary. We can always use another pair of hands.'

The small car rocked, groaning on its springs.

'Let's go,' said Jonathon.

* * *

Campbell lay, whey-faced, on the operating table.

'Can you handle the mask and chloroform?' Jonathan asked.

Already masked, Mary nodded. The patient's abdomen had been sterilized: she had checked the surgical instruments which Jonathon had gathered from the sterilizer; collected three bottles of saline solution and extra swabs which they might have to use to wash out the peritoneum, if the appendix had ruptured and contaminated the abdominal wall.

Campbell's entire stomach was rigid as a board: there were none of the usual intestinal gurgles and grumbles. Everything pointed at peritonitis. A major crisis in any hospital — let alone one that was closing down.

'Ready?' she asked.

'Angus,' Jonathon said gently. 'We're going to put a cotton mask over your face, to anaesthetize you. You won't feel a thing until you waken up.'

Campbell's agonized face twitched. 'This bit I remember well,' he said tightly. 'Do I count to ten?'

Jonathon patted his shoulder, then nodded to Mary.

She blanked her mind: focussed down. With her left hand, she gently positioned the mask over Campbell's face. Anaesthetizing by inhalation was a black art: there were no rules about how much chloroform should be given; simply enough to put the patient deeply asleep. And that varied from patient to patient, even when they seemed identical.

She carefully dribbled a few drops of chloroform onto the cotton mask: its odour filled the theatre. She watched it evaporate, dribbled a couple of drops more. Counted two minutes, giving time for the patient to inhale, go down deep. Instinctively, she dribbled another drop onto the mask.

Campbell's breathing steadied, slowed: his body relaxed. She reached forward, flicked open his eyelids.

No reaction.

'He's ready,' she said quietly.

Jonathon studied the sterilized abdomen: did his old student trick of measuring three fingers wide beneath the navel.

'Scalpel,' he said, and the instrument was instantly placed into his gloved hand. 'I'm making a bigger incision than usual. If the appendix is ruptured, we don't want to be constricted in cleaning out the peritoneum . . . maybe a five-inch incision. What do you think, Mary?'

She thought back: operating theatres in wet tents, mud everywhere; standing on duck-boards even in the theatre; the whine and crash of shells landing only fields away. No second chances for dying men.

'Six inches,' she said. 'We've both got big hands.'

* * *

Mary coped with the surgery as she had coped with the journey north: like an automaton. It was hours later, in Chrissie's house, when everything suddenly threatened to overwhelm her. She got up and left Aggie sprawled across the floor playing with Tommy. Pulling her jacket tight, she walked aimlessly through the streets. In any fishing village, all roads lead ultimately to the harbour, and she found herself hurrying mindlessly down the final slope.

Perhaps it was the slope: more likely her state of mind. Her hurrying footsteps broke into a trot. Then a run. Mary found herself racing along under the sea wall of the harbour, tears streaming down her cheeks.

She stopped at the end of the quay, her breath coming in shuddering gasps. The wind from the sea gusted round her: rough and impersonal yet an essential element of home. Mary pulled back her hood, let her hair stream out behind. As she breathed in the keen, cold air, her tears slowly stopped.

She felt utterly bereft, abandoned. Turning slowly, she saw the pile of old nets were still there, waiting for mending: where she had first seen Neil, huddled and lost to his demons, as she was now lost to hers.

How could he have done this — coldly and calmly removing the one thing she wanted in life: himself. Rejecting the only thing she was sure about: their love for each other. She felt as if her heart would break — an almost physical sense of pain.

She'd thought she knew the way ahead. Not any more.

In her mind, she recognized that one small part of what he'd said was true: she had a gift for medicine. But he'd set the target higher than she would ever have dared set it for herself. She could be a nurse: take all the classes, read the books, to formalize her qualification.

But a doctor? Worse, a woman doctor? Only college girls did that.

9

'He keeps it neat, this place.'

'What? Sorry?' Aggie turned, startled.

'The hospital,' Campbell said patiently. 'Your doctor keeps it neat.'

'Jonathon? Neat? He doesn't know one end of a duster from the other — but, yes, this hospital is the apple of his eye.' She came over to Campbell's bed. 'Is everything fine? Will I get the nurse for you?'

'I thought you were the nurse,' he smiled.

'Me? No, I'm only helping. Mary's our nurse. She worked in front line hospitals, right through the war. Over in Belgium and France.'

'So why's she here, with qualifications like that?'

'Buckie's her home. She was a gutter, like me, before the war. After she finished working in an English convalescent hospital, she came back.'

'Weren't you both walking with these fisher-women?' Angus Campbell was still trying to sort out the half-remembered fragments of that night.

'That's right. We'd all travelled up over-night from Yarmouth.'

'Yet she came straight here?'

'Jonathon needed her.'

'Hmm.' Campbell frowned. 'Isn't there a full-time nurse?'

'With the hospital closing, he'd to pay her off. But she's not as good as Mary, It's Mary he always turns to when he needs real nursing help.'

Aggie tried to stifle the familiar ache of jealousy. Failed.

Campbell's fingers played restlessly with the bed sheet.

'How long has your doctor been looking after this town?'

'Ever since he qualified. When he joined the practice, straight from medical school, our old doctor was almost seventy. It was meant to be a long apprenticeship. But Dr Fredericks took poorly and became one of Jonathon's first patients. Jonathon was thrown into the deep end. Dr Fredericks watched, and judged, then handed over the practice to him, just before he died.'

'So he's good, this Jonathon?'

'The very best there is.'

The vehemence of her reply made Campbell smile. 'Even if he doesn't know one end of a duster from the other?'

Aggie laughed. 'Pay no attention to me. I grew up with Jonathon — I'm the last person in the world to take him seriously . . . '

Campbell nodded. 'I've a sister back in Canada, who treats me just the same. She's got a clutch of kids around her now, but she still reckons that she could out-run, out-gun, and out-climb me.'

'Good for her,' said Aggie.

Campbell's smile faded. 'He has to be good, or I wouldn't be here. Out where I come from, a burst appendix is usually a killer. Unless we can get people to a big hospital. This Jonathon of yours is one heck of a doctor . . . '

'He's one heck of a man,' said Aggie. Then blushed, and began to chase non-existent dust.

This went deeper than sibling rivalry, Campbell thought wryly.

'Yet his hospital is closed, apart from me,' he said. 'What's the problem? Why are you shutting down, when you have people of the calibre of your doctor and your nurse?'

'Bad luck,' said Aggie. 'A local man gifted this building to the town, then forgot to change his will. Now his relatives want the money.'

'It happens. But why not raise the cash yourselves? Give them the money, and keep your hospital?'

'Believe me, we tried. All we can raise is

goodwill — there's no money in the town. Not after years of war and poor fishings.'

'Campbell nodded. 'That's what my grandfather says. But he was talking of Portgordon.'

'They'll have suffered just the same as us, and places like Findochty and Portknockie too. We've all got fewer boats chasing fewer herrings and are struggling to keep going. But it will get worse still — when this place closes down, that will hurt these fishertowns who have been using us. We'll be back to where we were before our cottage hospital, with people dying before they can get to Elgin or Banff. People forget — but I remember just how bad it was back then.' Aggie straightened Campbell's sheets and plumped up the pillows. 'Want a cup of tea?' she asked. 'That's about all I'm trained to do.'

'Could you make real coffee?' Campbell asked, with longing.

'What's coffee?' Aggie replied.

'That's what my grandma said,' sighed Campbell. 'Tea will do.'

* * *

'Is the Wee Man sleeping?' asked Chrissie, looking up from her knitting.

'He's out like a light.' Aggie flopped wearily into her seat.

Chrissie's needles clicked. 'You're doing far too much,' she scolded.

'Tommy's a full-time job — and you're more used to that than me.'

Chrissie's needles clicked steadily. 'Well, now that the fishing's over until April, you'll soon get back into the way of things.'

Aggie frowned at the fire. 'I hate being away,' she said. 'I'm missing his childhood. Every time I come home, he's inches taller. A proper boy now — I can't believe he'll be at school next year.'

Her daughter was in danger of missing more than her son's childhood, Chrissie thought. She was missing her own best years. Chrissie sighed: if only she could find a loon who could see past the boy, to the woman.

'That's the third time you've made a noise like a burst balloon,' Aggie accused her. 'What's up?'

Chrissie changed tack. 'What's got into Mary?' she asked, pulling wool from the ball. 'I've never known her so quiet . . . so listless. What's been happening, down at Yarmouth?'

Aggie shrugged. 'She's had a falling-out with Neil,' she said.

'Over what?'

Aggie hesitated. 'He wants her to aim high, to become a doctor.'

'A woman doctor? I've never heard the like!'

'Why not?' Aggie shot back. 'There's women doctors in most big cities nowadays. It's high time that women's problems were dealt with by a woman, and not a man.'

Chrissie reached the end of her row. 'Why should what Neil said have left her depressed? Is she sweet on him?' No reply. She stared over her specs at her daughter. 'Well?' she demanded. 'Is she?'

'Is she what?' asked Aggie innocently.

'I thought she was going to be Jonathon's nurse,' said Chrissie.

'With no hospital, is he going to need a nurse?'

Chrissie's hands paused. 'I suppose not.'

She waited, but her daughter had retreated into silence. Chrissie frowned, simultaneously pleased that her daughter could guard a confidence, and irritated that she wouldn't tell it to her mother.

So Mary was sweet on Neil. And Neil was telling her to aim high, and be a doctor. Higher than what? A wife to himself? Chrissie's needles clicked busily. If Mary's heart lay elsewhere, then it wasn't tied to Jonathon. Who had spent half his childhood in this very house: with Aggie spending the other half of their childhood in his.

So frustrating: without stirring from her chair, she could find a perfect wife for Jonathon — and a perfect man for her daughter. They were made for each other, for the long haul of life's ups and downs. There was only one thing missing. Where there should be a spark of electricity, of romance, there was only what there had always been — easy-going affection. Pity about that.

Chrissie sighed.

'You're making that noise again!' snapped Aggie.

* * *

Eric rose from the fish crate where he'd been sitting. The ship he'd been watching out for over two long days was finally steaming in from the east.

He'd recognize her anywhere: the *Endeavour*. Knocking out his pipe against his heel, he studied her keenly. Riding high and fast, as she should be doing, with no fish in her hold. No sign of damage. Then, as she turned into the harbour, he saw the patch of fresh paint along her waterline.

They'd known their trade, and made a good job of it, he thought.

Unhurriedly, he walked into the inner harbour, catching the warps that Johnnie threw up. Dropping each of them in turn over a rusty bollard, he fought down the urge to refill his pipe. Why should he be nervous?

Grasping the hoop at the edge of the pier, he swung his foot over onto the first rung of the vertical ladder. 'You've taken your time,' he called down to Johnnie. 'I was nearly sending out a polisman, to look for you.'

'Archie McCulloch, on that bike of his?' grinned Johnnie.

'Why not? With your steering, she's more likely to be piled up on dry land than out at sea.'

Eric's gruff banter made the deckhand's smile broader.

'Well, it was you that taught me, Skip.'

'Then you couldn't have been listening.' Eric gripped the hand that was offered. 'I've never been so glad to see a crew of wasters in my life.'

'It was touch and go,' Johnnie said soberly. 'Neil pulled us through.'

'Aye. Neil and the rest of you. He said on the telephone that he was proud of you. No panic. You just did what you had to do, like men.'

Johnnie shrugged. 'Neil and Andy are in the deckhouse, Eric.'

Eric grinned. 'Scared to come out?'

Johnnie laughed. 'We've all felt the rough edge of your tongue.'

'Not this time.' Eric climbed the steps and opened the door to the deckhouse. Andy was wearing a turban of bandages, hair curling out from underneath. He wouldn't, or couldn't, meet his father's eye. 'Well, well,' said Eric. 'The wanderers return.'

'I'm sorry, Da,' blurted Andy. Eyes on the floor.

'What for? What did you do wrong? Hitting timber out at sea on a dirty night — that's every skipper's nightmare. Your luck was out, that's all.'

Andy shook his head, winced. 'It was Neil that saved us,' he said.

'Neil only did what you would have done — if you hadn't had your senses scattered. Is it a new winch we're needing, after that?'

Andy's face came up, with a wan grin.

Eric walked to him. Gripped him by the arms. 'Don't you ever apologize to me again,' he said fiercely. 'For it was me that taught you, and I taught you to be the best there is. Get that head of yours mended — and the ribs. Then get out there and do what you've been taught to do. Bring back the top catches of herring to the port.'

'Right, Da,' said Andy. 'I'll do that.'

The words were important, badly needed.

For themselves, and for their more crucial implicit message. His da still had faith in him. For Andy, that sound old man's faith was priceless. Clumsily, he clapped his father's shoulder, then slipped out through the deckhouse door.

'He did nothing wrong,' said Neil. 'The boat's as good as new.'

'I know he did nothing wrong,' Eric said. 'But I'll tell you this — I'm glad I sent you out, to watch over him. Or I would be one son less, and the town would be in mourning for eight lost Buckie loons.'

'We made it, anyway,' Neil grunted.

He glanced up at the quay. Looking once, then twice, then once again for the figure he didn't want to see. But there was only Buckie harbour: a mess of boats and fishermen and busy colliers. Not a quine in sight.

'I'll get my gear,' he said, leaving the deckhouse.

Eric lingered, where he had stood for many days and nights before, staring through the salt-stained windows. Eyes that could see the silver gleam of herrings in the water half a mile away, had seen something else.

The brief look of utter desolation on his son's face.

Only a woman, missing, could put that there.

* * *

'We need to talk,' said Jonathon, sitting down on Campbell's bed.

'We do indeed,' the Scots-Canadian replied.

'You're healing nicely — no more tenderness than can be expected, blood pressure and temperature sound. You're fit enough to be transferred to Banff. I can drive you there this afternoon. They have a bed for you, and are happy to handle your convalescence. I'd rather keep you here — now that the girls are back, there's no problem with nursing — but . . .'

Campbell nodded. 'But you have to clear out your patients, then the beds, the theatre equipment, and whatever stores are left. In short, you need to empty the building, so that it can be put up for sale.'

'That's it, in a nutshell,' Jonathon smiled.

Campbell's face grew stern. 'Well, you disappoint me.'

Jonathon straightened. 'Why? Is something wrong?'

'Yes. Badly wrong. Why are you selling the place?'

'Because we have no choice.'

'Why can't you buy the building, leave it as it is? The local hospital?'

Jonathon fought down irritation. 'Because

we have no money.'

'Then raise it. From the people who will use the hospital.'

'We tried. We've barely raised enough to buy a new front door key.'

A slight smile twitched on Campbell's face. 'Perhaps you've been asking the wrong people?'

'We asked everyone — far and near,' Jonathon said simply.

'No. You didn't ask me. And I'm offended.'

The words were spoken quietly. So quietly, Jonathon wondered if he had misheard.

He studied Campbell, weighing what he knew of the man. Was this in jest? If so, it was in the poorest of taste. Somehow, that didn't fit the picture he was building of the recovering patient.

They could hear Aggie's voice, singing in the other ward. The cleaning regime went on, until the place ceased to be a hospital: that's what both women had decreed.

An émigré Scot, from Canada. A bell went off in Jonathon's mind.

'When your family emigrated to Canada, did they own little more than the clothes on their backs?' he asked.

'We were flat broke. My dad was laid off, after years of bad fishing.'

'And you're an outdoor man — anyone can

see that from your face.'

'I am.' Campbell's eyes were twinkling. He was enjoying this.

'Do you have anything to do with trees?'

'I spend my life among them.'

Jonathon's heart was beating as if about to burst from his chest. 'You didn't, by any chance, know Andrew Carnegie?'

'A grand old man,' said Campbell. 'A tough old son-of-a-bitch when you were dealing with him on business. But a heart of gold. Yes, I was truly privileged to be his friend.'

Jonathon shook his head. 'You can't be . . . ' he said weakly.

'I am.' Campbell grinned. 'I caught a first-class berth a couple of days before the Foundation's letter. On impulse. Left them to tell you I might be dropping in. I decided I was due a vacation. To visit the Old Country, meet my grandparents, see the place my mom never forgot.'

His smile became rueful. 'I didn't bargain on researching your hospital quite so closely. But you run a sound little outfit here. Good doctor, good nursing staff, good reputation. My grandparents tell me that it's the mainstay of . . . what did they call them? . . . the 'fishertoons'.'

'Well, I'm damned,' Jonathon said weakly.

'Quite the opposite,' Campbell said. 'How

much are the lawyers asking for this place?'

Jonathon told him. Crossing his fingers, below the level of the bed.

Campbell nodded. 'I'd be disappointing Andrew if I didn't bargain them down from there,' he said briskly. 'Right, cancel all plans to evacuate the building. Your hospital equipment — and myself — are going to stay right here. You too. But first, I'm going to need a lawyer . . . '

He grinned. 'This bit of hospital business, I am going to enjoy . . . '

* * *

Still dazed, Jonathon walked into the empty women's ward, where Aggie and Mary were cleaning under the beds.

'Oh, it's you,' said Aggie, glancing up. 'I saw the legs and thought it was somebody important.'

Jonathon towered over them. 'Stand easy, slaves. I'm going to make us all a cup of tea,' he announced.

Aggie sniffed suspiciously. 'Has he been drinking?' she asked Mary.

Mary rocked back onto her heels, head to the side. 'He looks sober,' she judged.

'Does this offer stretch to biscuits with our tea?' Aggie asked hopefully.

'Say the word, and I will run down to the town, and buy some.'

'Consider it said,' Aggie replied. 'And there are witnesses.'

Jonathon sat down heavily on one of the empty beds.

'Hey! I've just straightened these sheets,' Aggie complained.

'You will never guess who I've been talking to,' Jonathon said.

'There's only Angus Campbell through there.'

'Wrong. That's our fairy godmother, who is lying through there.'

'A fairy godmother with stubble?' Aggie queried.

'Why is he our fairy godmother?' Mary asked, rising from the floor.

'Behold this place,' said Jonathon. 'Everything that you see is ours: the beds, the chairs, the walls, even that old damp stain on the ceiling.'

'He *has* been drinking,' Aggie sighed.

'Angus Campbell is a friend of Andrew Carnegie. *The* friend, the one the Foundation asked to help. He has seen us, likes us, and is helping. He wants a lawyer, a banker, and his chequebook. He is buying the building from Johnnie Meldrum's heirs. Then giving it to the town — all threats removed, all documents signed and sealed.'

He smiled at Aggie: 'You may close your mouth,' he said benignly.

She did, with a click. 'He's doing what?' she asked.

'You heard.'

'But I don't believe.'

'Feel free. Believe. This place is ours.'

Jonathon suddenly swooped down, lifted her from the floor, and started dancing round the space between the beds with her.

'Stop it, you daft idiot,' she laughed.

It felt good, so good, to have his arms around her — even in fun. And good to see in his laughing face the boy she had always known.

'Stop it,' she repeated. 'Angus Campbell will change his mind, if he sees us behaving like this.'

'I don't care,' said Jonathon. 'Well, I *do* care, if it's going to cost us the hospital. A day ago, we had no future. Now — or within a couple of weeks — we need never worry again about losing our hospital.'

He turned, gripped Mary's shoulders, shaking her gently. 'We can throw open our doors to patients again! We can plan, think through what we need to do to turn this place into a modern hospital. Go back round local businesses and local people to raise funds for new beds, new equipment — even new paint, once we've got everything else we need. This place is ours!'

It was impossible not to be caught up in his enthusiasm.

'Whoever would have thought . . . ' said Mary. 'We did no more for Angus Campbell than we'd have done for anybody. No bowing, or scraping: just treating him like an ordinary man.'

'That's what he likes,' Jonathon said, more soberly. 'We had no cause to try and impress him. He was just a stranger, somebody we could have done without, when we were closing down. But we put our own plans aside and dealt with his emergency. Then nursed him back through the effects of the anaesthetic and his early recovery. Without making a special fuss over him, because we didn't know that he was in a position to help us.'

'If we'd known, I'd have put extra sugar into his tea,' said Aggie.

'But you didn't — that's the whole point.' Jonathon smiled down at Mary. 'Well,' he said. 'An hour ago, I had nothing to offer. Now there's a job for both of you, if you want it. Head nurse for you, Mary. Trainee nurse and chief tea-maker for you, my quine. Neither of you need ever gut a fish again.'

He pointed a quivering finger at Aggie. 'But *you* will have to do what you're told by me,' he warned.

'No chance!' scoffed Aggie. 'Are you serious? About the job?'

'Cross my heart and hope to die,' said Jonathon.

'More to the left,' she ordered.

'Wrong. Your heart, contrary to popular belief, is under your sternum — your breastbone. In the centre of your chest. That's your first theory lesson.'

Aggie ran her hands over her hair, realization dawning. 'I'd never have to leave wee Tommy on his own again!'

'Then I've got one nurse?'

'As of now,' she said. 'When do we get paid?'

Jonathon laughed. 'When there's money. What about you, Mary? We can find a way to let you study nursing. I can help you with the book side of things, give you all the clinical training you need. You can sit, and pass, your nursing qualification in a couple of years.'

The light died in Mary's eyes. She frowned.

'Jonathon, can I think about that for a bit?' she asked.

Surprised, he said: 'Of course you can, my dear. But you are central to every plan I have, for this place. We need a good nurse. That means you.'

Mary's shoulders drooped.

'I'll wash my hands and make the tea,' she said.

* * *

Frowning, Jonathon watched her leave. 'I thought she'd jump at my offer,' he said. 'She's not still thinking about that crazy doctor idea, is she?'

'Who says it's crazy?' Aggie demanded.

Jonathon shook his head. 'Doesn't she realize that she will have to study to get into medical school? Then seven long years after that, including her clinical experience? She could be in her thirties by the time she qualifies — *if* she ever lasts the pace, and passes her examinations. You don't just *wish* to be a doctor. It takes years of study.'

'She knows all that.'

'Ah well,' Jonathon said. 'No point in crossing bridges until we come to them. First things first. We have our hospital back! I feel like dancing . . . madam, will you do me the honour of this dance?'

'I certainly won't,' said Aggie primly.

Then she was picked up and whirled into something which might have been a lively waltz — or a drunken polka, or just about anything. No point in trying to guess which steps came next. She left her feet to look after themselves, and hung on for grim death.

'Sorry!' he said, tripping over her, for the umpteenth time.

She hauled him to a stop.

'Jonathon!' she said firmly. 'You've got two left feet.'

'It's the orchestra. They're an absolute disgrace.'

'I don't hear any orchestra,' she said, still in his arms.

'Exactly. They should be playing louder — and in tune . . . and all at the same time . . . ' Jonathon's voice gradually tailed off.

They were standing very close, in each other's arms. Smiling.

Somehow, without knowing who made the first move, they were kissing. Gently, almost in surprise. Then intensely, with real passion.

Jonathon finally eased her away. 'What happened there?' he asked nobody in particular. Then his hand came up to touch the dark curl on Aggie's neck. 'That curl,' he said. 'It's been haunting me. It's perfect. Your neck is perfect. In fact . . . ' he turned her slowly round at arm's length, ' . . . the rest of you is pretty perfect too. When did it happen,

Aggie? When did you become this beautiful woman?'

She curtsied. 'Thank you, kind sir.'

Then the words were out, before she even knew that they were there.

'Is this a leap year?' she asked.

'I don't think so,' he replied. 'Why?'

'Pity. Because, if it was, I was going to ask you to marry me.'

Jonathon stared at her. Somewhere in the old house, an old clock was ticking slowly: the only sound in the place.

'Shouldn't you get down on one knee, or something?' he asked.

'I'll get down on two, if it makes any difference.'

Jonathon studied her, then a slow smile broke on his face. 'That's it,' he said. 'I've just solved a problem that has puzzled me for years. I have always loved you — that's why I've never looked at any other woman.'

He scooped her up into his arms and strode out of the ward.

'Where are you going?' she gasped, clinging to his neck.

'Through to see Angus Campbell. To show him that he's bought me a wife as well as a hospital.' Jonathon smiled. Then looked down on her. 'But you'll still have to make the tea,' he warned. 'No special privileges.'

'It's a deal,' said Aggie, burying her face into his neck.

* * *

The wind from the sea was bitingly cold. Mary wrapped her shawl more tightly round her head and shoulders. Only seven months before, she had hurried down this slope towards the harbour, joy in her heart: because at last she had come home, to pick up the threads of her life again. Now her step was slow, and her heart was heavy.

So much had happened, in between.

The harbour was deserted. At the end of the winter fishing, the men were back with their families, taking things easy for a bit. After the New Year had passed, the harbour and its shipyards would be full of life again, as boats were winched up and repaired, getting ready for the year ahead. Until then, the drifters were moored two and three deep around the quays.

Mary walked slowly under the harbour wall then stopped, looking down at the solitary figure below. Sitting on the raised edge of the hold, hunched over the pad on his lap: drawing something that existed in his mind alone, because his head never came up, to check the subject.

'I thought I'd find you here,' she said.

His face lifted: his eyes, which were the colour of the sea, quiet and guarded. 'Mary Cowie,' he said.

The hairs on her neck tingled, each time he spoke her name like that.

'What are you drawing?' she asked.

'Scribbling. Just passing the time.'

Mary dropped the shawl from her head. 'I didn't come down to see you land from the south,' she said. Having had to fight herself to stay away.

'I wasn't looking for you,' he lied.

They studied one another: he made no effort to climb the ladder to the quay; she didn't ask to come down, because it was bad luck for any woman to step on any fishing boat. Although her own luck could scarcely be worse.

'Jonathon's offered me the nurse's job,' Mary said.

He waited, then asked: 'And?'

'I'm thinking about taking it.'

'Why?'

'Because I want to stay here, in this place. With my friends.'

And you, she added silently.

'Wrong decision,' he said quietly. 'You're a fighter. A fighter should always fight, not hide away. What's happened to the fire that was in your belly? Your hunger to be a pioneer? One of the first women doctors?'

'That doesn't matter anymore,' she said.

'It does. Deep down inside. I can see its flame.'

She dropped her head, unable to hold his gaze.

'There is an alternative,' she began.

'Which is?'

Despite the biting cold, Mary's cheeks burned. 'I could study, through in Edinburgh, Try to get into Elsie Inglis's hospital, to be trained with the other college girls. Study for years, just to catch up with them. Then study to become a doctor. When I don't know if I have the brains — or the courage — to finish the job. And I would never know where the money to buy my next meal was coming from.'

He watched her silently.

'Come with me,' she said. 'Come back to the city, to study art.'

'Me? Leave my own people and my work behind? I'm born to be a fisherman — not to stake my future on a talent I've only just discovered.'

It was no more than the truth. She was asking him to come and share her sacrifices, and the risk that everything might easily be in vain.

‘I need your courage,’ she said honestly. ‘I can’t do this on my own.’

‘Nor can you do it leaning on a broken reed,’ he told her grimly. ‘On a man who still can’t sleep, who gets the shakes. Who is afraid.’

‘We could be scared together. Help each other overcome our fears.’

She should be ashamed, a woman offering so openly to share her life with any man. But this wasn’t just any man: it was Neil, and she was driven by her fear.

Because there was more than studying which scared her. She had worked among these pioneers, and had no illusions about what she would be taking on. If she went to Edinburgh, it wouldn’t be just to enter medicine. It would be to move into the front line of politics, to fight in that other war; the war that had still to be won. The fight for women’s rights — where men were the main enemy. It was a bleak and lonely campaign: you couldn’t fight men for women’s rights, then go home to live with one. From what she’d seen, none of these fiery women warriors could sustain a relationship with a man.

But Neil was unique: the only man she knew who might understand the broader context, and support her; who could help her to define and guard a space which would be theirs alone.

Where she could be a woman, not just a warrior.

They could be the exception to the rule. Without him at her side, she would be condemning herself to loneliness, whatever her studies won.

Their eyes locked. In his face, she could read his indecision.

His eyes dropped, and he closed the child's exercise book he used for sketching. There was something utterly final in that gesture. 'I cannot tell you how honoured I am,' he said quietly. 'But she travels fastest, and furthest, who travels alone. I would be worse than a sea anchor to you. I would only drag you down.'

'A sea anchor saves lives in a storm,' Mary argued.

'As you will. But first, you must become a doctor.'

The wind ate into her bones. She felt old, and cold. Unwanted. Pain and tears were welling up, from deep inside.

'Then it's no?' she asked, fighting them.

He stood silently. Mary lifted her shawl, automatically covering her head again, and walked leadenly from the harbour.

'Because I love you too much to say 'yes','

he finally replied. When he knew she was gone, and would never hear him.

He opened the exercise book with fingers that shook, and found the page where he'd been working. A young woman's face, tilted slightly, looking directly at the artist, laughing. There was wind in her hair, teasing it from her face, giving it movement and life. A sparkle of light and humour in her eyes. For the first time, he had caught light, and set it down on paper.

It was Mary's face. All that he would have of her to remember.

* * *

It had rained all morning, and was raining still. A small grey rain that stung with the intensity of its cold. Down over the harbour, Mary could hear the seagulls calling endlessly. For many years, the sound of home.

She looked along the station platform. Two or three knots of people waiting for the Aberdeen train. Huddled together for warmth, their umbrellas up and slanted against the endless Buckie wind.

She was on her own. Sneaking off, like a thief, because she couldn't bear the thought of having to say goodbye to anybody. Up at the water tower, she saw the engine taking on water, steam swirling round its wheels.

She wished Aggie well. Wished her and Jonathon all the joys that life could offer — joys that would never now be hers.

Once again, she was leaving home — her future stark and uncertain: heading south to Edinburgh with barely enough in her purse to cover a couple of months' accommodation. Bruntsfield Hospital: she had heard so much about the place. Were they still training women doctors? Would they take her in, as a student? How would she earn the money to keep herself there?

What if they shook their heads and closed the door on her?

She couldn't stay here, whatever happened. Not now. Once Buckie had been her home. Now, she had no home. Her heart ached.

Mary looked down at her small case, which held much less than her kitbag as a gutter quine had done. Like Dick Whittington: she was travelling with little more than he had carried at the end of a stick, when he set out to make his fortune. The thought brought a wry smile. No bells for her.

With a hiss of steam and clank of metal wheels, the train slid into the station platform. Her hand on the door handle of an empty compartment, she took one last look around. People entering their compartments, shaking water from their folded umbrellas. A young couple: she leaning out through the open compartment window, he straining up to her for one last kiss. She hoped life would be kind to them.

She should have dropped in on Gus, to say goodbye: but she didn't have another goodbye left in her — and she could only hope that Aggie would understand. She would miss her strength, her lively sense of humour.

Mary opened the compartment door and climbed in. Closing the door, she lifted her case onto the string cradle of the luggage rack, and sat down beside the window. Steam hissed out around her feet, bringing sooty-smelling heating to the carriage.

Outside, the guard's whistle shrilled. Mary half rose to let the window down, for one last look. At the town, of course, but also at the empty platform, hoping for the miracle that would never happen: the sight of him coming at the last minute to bring her home. She made herself sit down.

The carriage jolted, then moved, amid dense clouds of steam. Far in front, she could hear the chug of the engine, the metallic scream of its wheels spinning, as they fought for traction. Through the drifting steam, the platform passed quicker and quicker.

Then the figure of a man came running; looking into each compartment window in turn. Her door was wrenched open. A kitbag sailed in across the dirty floor, then the man came hurtling through behind it, landing on all fours, rolling across her feet. Outside, a stream of invective as the stationmaster cursed, then slammed the door closed as it passed him.

Neil looked up, soot smudged across his face.

'You took your time,' she said. Her heart racing.

'I couldn't find my pencils. I've had to leave them all behind.'

He reached up a hand, and she braced herself, nurse-style, to help haul him to his feet. 'Did you change your mind?' she asked.

'About coming, yes. About you, no. Never.'

His hand turned, until their fingers were gently laced together.

First the town, then the countryside, sped past. She couldn't speak.

'Somebody had to see you off,' he said at last. 'Make sure you caught the proper train in Aberdeen. Make sure you found yourself some decent digs, in Edinburgh. Then make sure that there's food on the table, for you coming home at night. Unless I'm drawing, and forget about everything else.'

'For how long?' she asked breathlessly.

'For as long as it takes.'

'What if we starve?'

'Then we starve together. Only, we won't. I'll find a job, to put you through the college. And put food on our table.'

'What if it takes seven years for me to be a doctor?'

'It will take six, part-time, for me to become an artist. Maybe longer.'

'Race you,' she said, her heart singing, bursting with joy. 'Like we used to race as kids, from boat to boat, across the harbour.'

'You always won. I let you win.'

'You never did!'

'I stayed behind you, in case you fell into the water.'

Somehow, in the rocking carriage, they were in each other's arms.

'What did your dad say? And Andy?' she asked breathlessly.

'I didn't have time to tell them.'

'Why not?'

'Because I wasn't coming. Right up until I saw your engine at the water tower. And knew that in ten minutes' time, you would be travelling out of my life forever. I couldn't bear the thought. So I just followed my heart and my feet, raced home, threw some clothes and my sketch pads into my bag, and ran for the station. I nearly didn't make it.'

She hugged him tightly. 'And I was crying,' she said. 'It felt as if my heart was breaking. I think I would just have got out of the carriage at the next station, and caught the first train home.'

He kissed her fiercely. 'Waste of a ticket, that,' he said. 'See? I've saved you some money already . . . '

We do hope that you have enjoyed reading this large print book.

Did you know that all of our titles are available for purchase?

We publish a wide range of high quality large print books including:
Romances, Mysteries, Classics
General Fiction
Non Fiction and Westerns

Special interest titles available in large print are:
The Little Oxford Dictionary
Music Book
Song Book
Hymn Book
Service Book

Also available from us courtesy of Oxford University Press:
Young Readers' Dictionary
(large print edition)
Young Readers' Thesaurus
(large print edition)

For further information or a free brochure, please contact us at:

Other titles published by Ulverscroft:

ANOTHER CHANCE, ANOTHER LIFE

Mark Neilson

In a cruel yet comforting parallel, friends Becky and Kathy have recently both lost their jobs, and face the prospect of starting their lives all over again. Taking up the offer to borrow her elderly uncle's narrowboat, Becky sets sail for the Yorkshire Dales with her son Jonathon, wondering if new pastures might help her regain what she's lost. Meanwhile, Kathy finds herself in love with a widower whose only daughter is still in mourning for her lost mother — her grief proving a solid opponent to any new woman in her father's life . . .

A STRANGE INHERITANCE

Mark Neilson

Everybody dreams of a surprise inheritance . . . Meg is at her lowest ebb when she finds that her uncle, Henry Waterston — who she never even knew existed — has left her a derelict windmill in a Yorkshire dale. With the gift comes a strange final request, asking her to 'help close the circle'. Meg visits the mill, falls in love with the place and throws herself into the challenge of rebuilding the old business. In the process she finds new friends — and a new love. But who exactly was Henry Waterston, and why did he leave Meg everything he owned?